Death On The Downs

An Inspector Daffyd Jones Novel

By
Diana Anstead

CHAPTER ONE

As he walked along the Brighton Esplanade tapping the blue railings, Inspector Jones was not watching the waves crashing up the pebbly beach he was remembering the day he told Barbara of his promotion and asked her to marry him and move down South to start a new life together. Suddenly he stopped as the memories of that moment crept into his thoughts and left him bereft of everything around him.as he grieved for his lost love. She had said she loved him but when the Sussex opportunity had come she had totally refused to consider moving down South. They had talked over marriage and she wore a diamond as proof of her love. They had discussed him possibly transferring to another police force away from Liverpool But Barbara always hesitated to commit to leaving her home area .He understood her need to be near her parents and to help with her handicapped brother. But he had needs too…

I needed to get away from the memories of Stan's murder. I had to have a fresh start. My father, my grandfather and now my good friend Stan were gone and I felt that I couldn't breathe….

He was still, almost frozen, remembering the time they had last spoken. After his move he tried to keep the relationship alive by going up north as often as he could and by numerous phone calls, but it soon became apparent that Barbara was not going to change her mind.

That final Sunday they arranged to meet in London Jones knew in the first minute together that it was hopeless. Barbara avoided his kiss and refused to take his arm as they walked along the Embankment.

He gripped the blue railing tightly remembering word for word their last conversation.

"Is this where you tell me we are through" he asked after they had found a table at their usual pub.

"Yes" she said, fiddling with her gloves.

"Any reason, other than the obvious one of distance?"

"Only that I want a boyfriend who is here with me when I need help with my parents, or with Tommy!"

"Is there anybody else in the picture?"

"No not really, at least not yet," she stammered as she got up to leave without touching her drink.

They had walked together, in silence to the station but she pleaded with him "Please don't come any further!" and ran quickly onto the platform and out of his life.

Jones pushed away from the railing and thoughts of Barbara and continued his journey through the small winding, streets that eventually would take him to the headquarters of the Sussex Police. As he walked he mentally assessed of how his first few weeks had gone.

His superintendent, Young, had been friendly and supportive yet still maintained that distance that traditionally occurred between the different ranks of officers.

"But I like him," thought Jones. "He seems fair, listens to officer's concerns and responds with encouragement. Despite the daily hustle Jones thought the station had a very positive, friendly atmosphere and functioned well as a team.

Inspector Daffyd Jones was a dark haired man who had inherited his Welsh forbearers height and strong build. All the men in his family were miners. His father and grandfather had worked side by side down the Cwmcarn colliery until a cave-in had killed both them and several others. Daffyd was just ten years old when the accident happened.

As a child he had been fascinated by the gigantic turning wheel that lowered the cage full of miners down the shaft to the coal seams. But since the day the men he loved had gone down the mine but had never come up Daffyd hated the view from his window and all things connected with coalmining. On that day he had determined that as soon as he could he would leave the village and go to England to be a policeman.

When the time came to leave his mother beseeched him to stay and marry a village girl, just like his brothers. But Daffyd wanted out. He loved his mam dearly but he felt trapped by the mountains. They had a claustrophobic effect on him, closing in on all sides around the few groups of houses that formed the village. He felt that the mountains served to keep the villagers in. enclosed in their little world. He saw the mountains as a barrier to growth, to progress and seemed able to stifle an individual's wish to move ahead.

Even at an early age he was aware that the owners of the coal mines owned the majority of property in each of the villages scattered up the valley. As he grew older he learned that his entire village was owned by a couple of families who kept the villagers in a type of bondage by owning everything and being the major employer. In fact the only employer. Even as a youth Jones experienced the unjust and demoralizing power held by the mine owners as his mother fought, vainly, to get compensation for the loss of her husband and father. The two families owned the land in the valley, built what was necessary and then rented houses and shops to local people. In his village they owned all the shops and the one hotel which was the only drinking establishment in the place. For all Jones knew they probably owned the school and the rugby field, but he wasn't going through his life forever lowering his eyes and doffing his cap like the men of his village.

Sgt Smith was already at his desk when Jones called out "Good morning" as he hurried into his own office. The working relationship between Jones and his veteran sergeant had been very tense at the beginning. Jack Smith had heard the talk about this hot shot, uppity youngster coming to Brighton and had already built up a resistance to any changes or so called efficiencies that this Jones fellow might want to establish. And Jones for his part had learned something about this veteran policeman who, although qualified had turned down promotion several times. Why? Nobody seemed to know. But gradually the ice between them had thawed. Perhaps because Jones had found that Smith's favourite pub was just a short walk away from the station and at the first opportunity had invited Smith to join him for a drink.

But this morning Jones had to prepare for his afternoon meeting with the local citizen's group and he knew he must be well prepared as it could turn very confrontational if he wasn't prepared with an answer for the many questions thrown his way. And besides the Chief Constable would be there. A man Jones had met and not liked.

"Dammit I was just getting into my report." Jones had grown increasingly angry and frustrated the previous afternoon as he worked through his notes on a nasty assault case and this tap on his door did not help his mood.

"I'm sorry to interrupt you Dai'" explained Supt Young, " but I've just had the C.C. on the telephone asking, well ordering me actually, to organize a meeting of the CID and local, influential citizens regarding these robberies that have been happening in our area. Apparently these people have been organizing themselves into small vigilantly groups who go out at night and patrol their communities, either by foot in the villages, or by car for the houses further afield. It has become awkward as they have recruited their local council person and their MPs complaining that we are not giving them enough attention." Supt. Young sat down heavily in the chair. "And now we have to deal with our Chief .Constable who has worked himself into quite a lather over this."

"You know how I hate these meetings. Just tell me when and where?" Jones knew he had no choice.

"Tomorrow afternoon, at the Town Hall. I will be there and together let's hope we can put a stop to these complaints. Bring the latest figures Dai let's see if we can baffle the politicians, at least, with facts and figures."

During the past months ten robberies had taken place in country homes in three different areas of the county. The items taken were small but valuable such as jewellery, silver pieces, gold and silver snuffboxes, items easily carried away and just as easily passed from hand to hand in a deal.

Each of the houses was set away quite a distance from their neighbours. Some houses were surrounded by woods and fields, some were protected by high walls and locked gates and in two instances had reliable security systems. The one house in Poynings actually had a man on the gate during the day and dogs loose in the grounds during at night but neither of these measures deterred thieves who entered the premises undetected. The houses in Steyning and Bramber were of a similar style with similar systems. One owner had a set of Georgian silver cutlery and all his silver candlesticks taken. In another house the thieves concentrated on a large set of Venetian glass paperweights, all thirty-five were taken. According to Sgt Smith these types of burglaries were unusual for the Sussex area.

"This style of operations happens closer to London. In Surrey or Kent and is usually done by a London gang who know enough of the criminal element down here to stay well away from our patch."

"Perhaps we have some new people down here. Perhaps we have imported some London low life looking for a softer touch than up in the Big Smoke," wondered Jones.

"Could be," agreed Smith," but why now, I wonder what has bought about a change?"

"How many known locals have we interviewed so far?" asked Jones

"There were fourteen possibilities on the list. We didn't include the older ones, mostly because they couldn't climb walls or gates or run quickly enough to clear the dogs. It really has to be someone physically fit, agile and would fit into the country community. We know that three of the fourteen are currently serving time and we have interviewed seven others."

"Any probables?" asked Jones.

"Oh yes, three fit the bill regarding fitness and past jobs. Two are newcomers to the area and Metro gave me their details. Apparently London grew too hot so they moved down here." Smith pointed to his list of names,

"Spenser lives in Haywards Heath and Maitland moved to the Whitehawk area, both have valid driving licenses and both own cars. The third possibility is Hillier and he lives in Bramber. I called his home several times but he refused to come in for an interview. Eventually I sent Masters out to fetch him but all Masters found was an empty house on a derelict small-holding. No person present and neighbours said that Hillier and a woman lived there but had recently left. Apparently late one night a lorry drove into their laneway and in the morning they and their belongings, were gone, nobody knew where. I checked the dates with the neighbours and it seems they were gone before the last two jobs."

"Well we will have to track him down anyway, put Masters back on it and get him to talk to everyone on the list even the older ones might know something. I wonder if any of those three knew each other." Jones asked.

"Not according to the interviews."

"Well Jack what is your gut feeling about this?"

"I'm sure we have the three most likely but there is something going on that I can't quite put my finger on."

"What do you mean?"

"Some of those on the original list were very nervous. Not just about being called in but more as if they were afraid of something else. As if somebody would hear about them being interviewed and there would be personal consequences. For instance young Binder, who now lives in Shoreham, was literally shaking in his chair and he's usually a cocky little punk but he was scared of something. There was a moment when he seemed ready to open up, give us some information. But suddenly he shivered and then just shut down as if terrified. He refused to answer any more questions. We did confirm his alibi for each night so it wasn't him but he knows something is up. Two of the others also hinted that somebody would be very annoyed at these robberies. But neither would say anymore. I wondered if one of them, new to the area, has unknowingly trespassed on somebody else's territory."

"I hope not," answered Jones, "that could get very violent."

The meeting at the Town Hall had been a lesson in both tedium and patience. Both officers knew that the citizens were mostly civic-minded people who wanted to help the police solve the crimes. But like similar meetings this one had been taken over by those with the loudest voices, who were, as always, the ones with the most complaints. Despite efforts from the chairperson to keep the meeting orderly there were several interruptions as speakers were shouted down. A great deal was said about lack of police services provided to small communities like theirs, about the competency of the force in general and, as was often the case, the citizens firmly believed that all the criminals were imported and that none of their children or acquaintances could possibly be guilty of a crime..

There was one man in particular who seemed to delight in making comments deriding the efforts of the local constabulary, referring to the said officers as being slow to act, out of touch with the youth and even going so far as to call the officers lazy.

“Really, what do you actually mean by that comment? Do you have any proof or are you just sounding off now that you have grabbed the floor?” Inspector Jones had had enough. “If you have solid proof of what you claim then I want to see it. Don’t be making criticisms about one of my officers without proof.” Jones voice had slipped into his natural Welsh lilt as he tried to contain his anger.

Throwing back his chair the man shouted at Jones, “Don’t talk to me like that. I’m a personal friend of the Chief Constable. Obviously you’re not from around here. I don’t know how you run things in Wales but here in England we do things properly,.” was the angry retort while other people told him to be quiet and stay in his seat.

Supt Young gently, but firmly grasped his Inspector’s forearm willing him to stay silent. After several seconds Jones gradually relaxed and just stared at the offending man. Eventually the meeting broke up with a lukewarm promise from the local MP that he would press Westminster for more funding for the protection of rural communities

“Be careful Dai that man Moore has powerful friends in London, so I’ve been told. Don’t make him an enemy.” Young said as they walked together back to the station.

“Well it’s too late, there is something about that man that just gets the hair on the back of my neck on edge. I usually have a pretty good instinct about people and this one is no good. I have a feeling that we are going to cross swords again.”

“Oh dear our Chief Constable wouldn’t like to hear you saying that.” Jones turned to look at Young but the Supt. had looked away hiding a smile.

. The desk sergeant had passed a message on to Jones that the manager of the local greyhound Race Stadium needed an officer to visit him. Neither officer was sure why but had been assured that it was very important. Mr. Aberdeen greeted them in the front foyer and led them to his office where another man waited.

“Inspector this is our solicitor Mr. Sackville-Smythe who represents us in all our financial and other dealings, “explained Aberdeen.

"Why exactly are we here today?" Jones asked after shakings hands.

"Inspector we have lost, as in died, six of our best dogs just this past weekend."

"Well we don't deal in dead dogs," answered Smith as he rose preparing to leave.

"Yes, yes I understand that but you see their owner has also disappeared in very strange circumstances, just a week ago and we don't like the coincidence." He continued "We, the organization, was hoping that perhaps you could look into the matter for us."

"You mentioned strange circumstances what do you mean by that?"

Sackville-Smythe took over the conversation, "Inspector Mr. Forest, the owner of the dogs, was a very rich man not only did he run a stable of racing dogs here but he owned a luxury flat in London, many antique cars and a luxury yacht which is usually berthed in Gosport. The strange thing is that his boat was found floating off shore near the Isle of Wight, nobody on board and nothing has been heard of Forest since. That was about a month ago."

"Is there an investigation regarding his disappearance?" asked Jones.

"Yes we reported him as missing but as he had no close relatives that we know of, there is nobody to push things along. The other thing is that we bill the dog owners every month for various expenses for the racing but last month his cheque bounced, which was most unexpected, After all Forest is a major shareholder in the Stadium. Another thing when the auditor came in last week he found there were hundreds of pounds missing," added Mr. Aberdeen. "So after much discussion we decided to call you in as we feel there is something strange going on."

Inspector Jones was silent for a few minutes then, "It is very unusual for us to investigate this kind of issue but perhaps we could help out on a few things. First of all with an official request we can investigate your missing yachtsman. Secondly would you supply us with a full list of your employees and their duties here, including any who have been fired or disciplined in anyway? Thirdly Mr. Sackville-Smythe would you dig deeper into Mr. Forest's financial dealings, for example where does his wealth come from and who does he deal with professionally, that is if he had any business dealings at all. Regarding the dogs the RSPCA will let you know what killed the dogs."

Turning to his Sgt "Is there anything else we can do Jack?"

"Well yes. I have been up here to the races a few times perhaps I could come back and do a little snooping on a race night?"

"Let me know and I'll arrange for you to have a full run of the place," said a delighted Aberdeen.

Jones rose, "Gentlemen we will certainly do what we can for you at our end and we'll get in touch with Hampshire police to see what they have on your Mr. Forest."

"This is a strange set of events," remarked Smith as they walked towards their car.

"It certainly is but I can also see their difficulty in knowing where to go for help. The solicitor seems to be a decent fellow, not uppish or stuffy as some solicitors are." Jones was very thoughtful as Smith drove. "Jack I'm just thinking that there are some strange things happening lately, the robberies, a missing sailor and six dead dogs, an empty yacht and a large amount of missing money." He settled down into his seat, "I wonder what tomorrow will bring."

CHAPTER TWO

For the past three years rumours had circulated among the criminal underworld that a man living on the south coast had accumulated a vast collection of precious jewels in payment for nefarious business dealings with people who had the wealth not to be inconvenienced by what they saw as the trivialities of the Customs and Excise rules.

Despite many attempts to learn the identity of the man and whereabouts of the jewels nothing was known. But one person had become obsessed with tracking down the treasure. He was known as The Boss. A criminal who had enough resources to buy information, to organize robberies and to pay others to execute his plans. A man whose true identity was unknown even to his most trusted associates. This man protected his identity by keeping communication to a minimum, using a variety of public telephone boxes was his favourite method of passing information. He seldom met face to face with his employees but when it was necessary he always sat in the darkest corner of the meeting place and wore one of his many disguises.

Recently the Boss had become exceedingly frustrated that despite spending hundreds of pounds he was no nearer to knowing the man or the whereabouts of the jewels. All he had were just tidbits of information and was seemingly at a loss on how to proceed when one day, quite unexpectedly, his luck changed.

As was often the case in the criminal fraternity a chance meeting in a local pub led to a conversation regarding the possibility of a meeting with The Boss. One of his associates had been enjoying a quiet drink when he was approached by a shabbily dressed, older man who certainly looked to be on his 'uppers'.

"I'm looking for The Boss and the barman said that perhaps you might know where I could find 'im," he said very quietly

"Well maybe, maybe not. Who wants to know?" the drinker casually asked.

"Me," whispered the old man. "I came down from Lambeth special to meet 'im as I have information he's looking for."

"Give it to me and I'll tell him."

"Not bloody likely," said the man from Lambeth. "You think I'm some kind of fool. I want to talk to The Boss. Tell him I have information about a certain gentleman and a certain package of jewels. But I want good money for it, 500 nicker that's my price." The other man leaned over the counter sipping at his beer and thinking about what to do next.

"Wait here while I make a 'phone call."

"Well be quick about it. I'm not waiting all night."

"This is more like it. What do you think, is he genuine?" the Boss asked when his man telephoned.

"Well boss he's very poorly dressed and looks ill. He was very confident that you would buy the information he has."

"What's he want for it?"

"Five hundred quid," was the reply. The Boss pondered this for a few minutes. It was a great deal of money especially if the information was no good. But if it was good then the prize would be worth far more than five hundred. He told his associate to meet the informer as planned and then drive him out to the Shepherd and Dog, for an eight o'clock meeting.

"I will wait at the pub for only fifteen minutes so don't be late."

Within a couple of minutes the man was back at the bar.

"Tell you what come back here tomorrow night, about seven o'clock. The Boss will be here then and will decide if your information is worth his money."

"Oh well it is. See you 'ere tomorrow and no funny business." The old man quickly left.

The Boss sat himself in the darkest corner of the back room long before the appointed time. He was dressed in a long black cloak style coat, with black trousers, black boots with a heel and black gloves. He kept his face hidden beneath the rim of his wide hat. One of his men stood by the door leading to the Saloon bar.

By seven thirty the pub was already noisy as the evening drinkers began to make their way in from the London trains. Evidently most of the drinkers knew each other as the bar was filled with greetings, handshakes and a great deal of back slapping. But that was not the case with an elderly man who walked in just before eight o'clock. He walked in alone, his driver had insisted on staying outside for a while. Nobody spoke to him and when he ordered his drink the barman had to ask twice what he wanted. Others looked at him but turned away with just the merest nod of acknowledgement. He lifted his frail body onto a barstool, grabbed his Guinness and just stared down at the counter. He wore a dark cap pulled down low over his face and a long army greatcoat. His shirt was frayed at the collar, his trousers had not seen a press in many weeks and on his feet he wore a pair of dirty plimsolls.

He nursed his drink and just sat hunched over not noticing his driver walk in and nod briefly to a watching colleague. Crossing over to the bar the second man briefly touched the old man's elbow, gave him chance to finish his drink, then led the way down a dark corridor to the back room. Grabbing his cane and lowering himself painfully from the bar stool the man from Lambeth shuffled out into the corridor and followed the man into the darkened room.

From the shadows the Boss grunted "Well," and negotiations began. The informant told them that he was retired and no longer in the business, owing to an accident that happened during his last job, pointing to his leg. He went on. "I wus always a good worker, always did what wus asked and never got caught. This last job was for someone I'd known for years but I fell off me ladder and that was the end of that."

"So?"

"Well this man always promised he would look a'ter his workers but he just left me, no money no 'elp at all and now my missus is took bad with her chest and I aint got nuffink left to look a'ter 'er with."

"Who is this man?"

"I tell yer when I sees the money," The old man moved closer towards the shadowy corner whispering, "I know this 'un was deep into the smuggling all sorts of stuff over the Channel and is still running stuff even now up in the Smoke."

He waited leaning on his stick, waiting for an answer, saying a silent prayer that he could close the deal.

Suddenly an arm reached out and a deep voice said. "Write the name and address down. If you are lying to me we will find you. I will meet your price and give you a hundred more for your absolute silence." The Boss hissed. "Is that understood?"

"Yerr, I know how to keep me mouth shut," said the old man indignantly as he took the pencil and scribbled down some words on the back of an envelope.

Hurriedly he picked up the fat envelope, stuffed with money, that had magically appeared on the table and saying a hurried "Thank you guv'." he scurried out of the bar as quickly as he could hobble and climbed into the waiting car. He knew that he had done a dangerous thing and had to get home, collect his wife and move up north to his cousin's isolated farmhouse before he was found out.

In the darkened room the Boss picked up the paper and read the name. He was absolutely speechless. There had never been a sign that things were not as they seemed. Suddenly his hand started to shake, the paper floated down to the table as he sat motionless, just staring ahead not seeing anything or anyone.

CHAPTER THREE

Gently Bobby inched the door inwards. Easing his slim body through the narrow opening he stepped into the kitchen and held the door for his two mates. Gliding across the floor Bobby soundlessly opened the checkered curtains just wide enough to let a sliver of outside light cut into the pitch-black room. Turning to ease the backdoor shut he confirmed that the latch was up, in readiness for a quick get-away.

Softly the black clad figures moved from the kitchen into the main entrance hall where they waited, listening for any unusual noise. Outside the storm was at its height as claps of thunder rolled noisily over the South Downs, then out across the Channel only to curl around and head for land once more. The jagged lightening dashed here and there searching for a way to escape the curved valley that lay between the Downs and the sea. But inside the large red brick house all was silent. Using hand signals the men confirmed their route upstairs. Watches were synchronized and the leader emphasized, by raising one-two-three black-clad fingers, that they had three minutes to get it done and be back in the kitchen. Then the men separated. Two swiftly climbed the broad, circular staircase while the third, Bobby, listened at each of the three doors in the entrance hall. Satisfied that he was alone, Bobby crept silently around the foot of the stairs and down the long hallway to the large reception rooms at the back of the house, again checking other rooms that he passed.

That was his job. Keep watch on the main floor, drive the get-a-way car and then dump it. He knew that in this mansion-style house with its modern alarm system there would be valuables, but seventeen year old Bobby Williams had explicit orders not to touch anything, not even to look, to keep his hands firmly in his pockets as he kept watch. One thing Bobby had learnt in his short experience as an apprentice criminal was not to ask questions, never ask names and even more importantly always follow instruction implicitly. Tonight he had been hired to drive to the railway station, pick up two men who would then give him instructions for the night's job.

Bobby had followed his orders to the letter but young Mr. Williams was, by nature, inquisitive and believed, like the Boy Scout he had been, in always being prepared. So before leaving home he had slipped his pencil-thin torch into his pocket.

He could see that the back rooms were sheltered by trees and he calculated that he had a couple of minutes to spare so felt quite safe in having a closer look at this rich man's possessions.

He touched, almost caressed, the gilded frames of paintings; he ran his hand over the silver tea service, even picked up the teapot to test its weight.

"Very nice," he murmured, "that would fetch a bob or two,"

He pretended to pull the bell-pull by the fireplace to summon the butler, and then grinned at the thought. Moving swiftly back into the hallway he checked his watch and decided there was still enough time for further explorations.

Another door led to an even larger reception room and swinging the minute light across the room Bobby spotted something that glittered.

It was a collection of small silver pieces, napkin holders and thimbles. Flashing his light around the room Bobby spotted several other collections, each on its own cherry wood, occasional table.

Bobby was a tactile person and loved to touch things, especially those made of gold or silver. He tried some thimbles on his little finger, he ran his fingers across the decorative sides of the silver napkin rings and then he spied the group of snuff boxes. He let out a muffled exclamation of delight. He was fascinated by these pieces; he loved their colour and the artistry in their decoration.

Although a young man of little formal education he had educated himself to the value of silver, gold and precious stones, for his ambition was to be a dealer in antiques. But now he was out of time.

He had a last look round, clicked off his torch and crept softly back to the kitchen to wait for the others.

Upstairs the men crept along the top hallway confident that the thick carpets and heavy curtains would deaden their steps. The rooms at the front belonged to the housekeeper, the nanny and the young children, all of whom were sleeping and were to be left alone. They wanted the master bedroom which was at the back and was, according to information, empty. Although the heavy double doors of the master bedroom were locked they posed no problem for the locksmith and within seconds they were in.

It was a large, impressive room, decorated with massive pieces of cherry wood furniture and draped with Victorian style soft furnishings. Several oil paintings hung on the walls and an antique white marble fireplace faced a silk covered canopied bed. The windows were draped in luxurious red velvet curtains and pulled together. The thieves knew their target was the wall safe concealed behind clothing in the dressing room just off to the left.

Silently, the leader slid the hung clothing from side to side searching for the small picture, that he knew, covered the wall safe. Finally he had it, hidden behind a man's beaver coat. The safe had a double security lock, with the probability of a third lock inside. It was a new model promoted as being burglar-proof, but Miller knew his business, one of the best in the south was his reputation. Tonight he had to open up the safe, and then close it after his colleague had removed whatever he was looking for, leaving no trace of entry. Quickly Miller pulled the necessary tools from a roll of cloth hidden inside his jacket. The soft whirring of the drill was covered by the thick, heavy furnishings of the room and within minutes the job was completed and the leather package found inside was quickly hidden inside a shoulder-style bag the Leader wore under his coat. Making sure the picture was hanging straight and the clothes were even on the pole they quietly closed the double doors and crept towards the stairs. Suddenly a child's cough broke the silence. They stopped! Another cough, then silence. No movement from the other rooms. They looked at each other and then went down, two steps at a time, fleeing into the kitchen and out through the open back door held open by Bobby.

They sped across the back lawn, jumped the small hedge, dashed across to the village pond to where they had parked their vehicle. Well hidden amongst those belonging to the villagers. Panting, they piled into the Hillman and within minutes were out on the coastal road heading west, putting miles between them and the house. It was three o'clock in the morning and the rain, aided by the incoming tide, was coming down in sheets. The men were silent, the only noise to be heard was the sound of the water smashing itself against the undercliff walk, then pulling hard on the shingle as it receded only to repeat the movement over and over again. High tide always brought rough seas especially during October and criminals always appreciated stormy, moonless nights.

But young Bobby was wired up; he was humming away and tapping out a rhythm on the steering wheel as he manoeuvred the vehicle through the downpour.

"Piece of cake," was his response to the Leader's concern. Bobby had chosen a spot near the railway station to park for the rest of the night and once the engine was turned off the two older men fell asleep. But Bobby was still humming away at some popular song while fidgeting with the car radio trying to find something worth listening to. Finally, he gave up and shuffling down in his seat slept the innocent sleep of the young.

By five am Napier was up and ready to move out as he wanted everybody and the car, away from the area before news of the robbery broke. Hustling the two men he reminded them, in the strongest language, of the dire consequences should any hint get out about last night's heist, emphasizing that should that happen the Boss could not guarantee their personal safety. Napier, the Leader, took a briefcase from the boot of the car, called out, "So long," and walked quickly across the road in the direction of the railway station.

Miller, the safe-cracker, was in no hurry to catch his train. At this time of day Southern Railway ran several trains every hour to London and he knew of a café just down North Road that did a working man's fried breakfast, cheap.

Bobby was starving but he had to get the car away from the station and dump it. Once the men were out of sight Bobby quickly left the station area behind driving north until he reached the crossroad at the beginning of the climb to Devil's Dyke. Turning left he headed west down the hill towards Shoreham. He looked across at the now calm, blue water of the Channel watching several boats creep slowly towards the harbour. Bobby planned to leave the car behind the old Cement works on the Steyning Road. Although many of the workers lived in the row of houses close by, it was common knowledge that the majority of workers drove in from Steyning and surrounding areas, meaning there would be many cars and motor bikes parked at the back, out of sight of the road.

The car he was driving was his, so yesterday he had cleared everything out of the vehicle that could be linked to him. Now he made doubly sure that everything was clean by wiping down the steering wheel, the gear shift and seat tops with a damp rag and then tearing off the license decal from the front window and those on the bumper. Finally he unscrewed the number plates. Only then did he walk away confident that it would be a long time before anyone noticed the abandoned car, and even longer before they found the owner.

Bobby had acquired the little Hillman from a friend in the car business. He had kept in under wraps in another friend's back garden, using it only on the few occasions when he and Pamela went out, just the two of them. His parents knew nothing about the car. They knew he didn't have a driving license so they assumed he never drove. Bobby had spent hours making sure the engine was reliable and that the inside was comfortable. He wasn't bothered about the outside paint as he enjoyed driving a car that looked like a wreck yet, in his estimation, drove like a Jaguar. Regretfully Bobby knew that his car was now a 'hot' one so it had to go, especially as he would be so generously compensated for its loss. With his bag slung across his shoulder he stepped up the grassy verge and followed the road along the banks of the Adur River until reaching the bus stop.

"At last," muttered Bobby as he saw the double decker coming. "Now for some of mum's breakfast and dad's questions, but I'll survive. After what I did tonight life is going to be good." still muttering as he swung himself onto the bus to Brighton.

Bobby enjoyed his breakfast especially now that he had satisfied his dad... Bobby knew his Dad would ask questions so he had his story straight long before he walked in the front door.

"I helped out at the Savoy; you know the flick down by the Palace Pier. A friend had told me that they needed men to clean up after a small fire, but it had to be done at night. So I helped out and took all night."

"Did you get paid?" asked his dad.

"Later today," Bobby answered.

"Well I'm glad you're doing something useful," muttered his dad, as he pulled on his work boots and walked out of the door. Bobby was relieved, his story had worked and if his dad asked again about the money he would have some to show him. Bobby ran upstairs to his bedroom and locked the door. He was feeling very pleased with himself. Despite all the dire warnings Bobby had pulled off his very own job last night.

Smiling he reached for his secret box hidden on top of his wardrobe. Gently from his bag he lifted out the four snuff boxes that he had stolen from the house in Rottingdean. He caressed them lovingly, turning each one over to look at the markings as he laid them on his pillow. Bobby was convinced that the four trinkets would be his entry into the criminal underworld. He had valuables to sell and a reputation to build. Some of his profits would go to keep his promise to his mates for a soccer weekend in London but the rest, the majority would be his. He put the boxes into his hiding place and then sat on the edge of his bed. Excitement welled inside him, he could hardly breathe.

Bobby was a young man who wanted money quickly but was not prepared to wait to earn it. No, he considered himself smart in the ways of the world and wanted his rewards quickly. Every time others on a job referred to him as The Kid, Bobby felt insulted and became more determined to make a name for himself. And that name could only come by building a reputation and earning the acceptance of others in the same line of business

"This is it" he yelled to his mirror," Just you watch me now! I am on the move. No longer just The Kid but Mr. Williams." He smiled "or Bobby to my friends." He fell down on his bed, hugging and punching his pillow as he rolled to and fro and quietly yelled, "I did it. Nobody knew. I Bobby Williams, formerly The Kid did it!"

CHAPTER FOUR

When Alex Moore had returned home he was immediately confronted by his housekeeper's reporting that four snuffboxes from his prized collection were missing. Mrs. Stevens was exceeding upset and felt that she had failed in her responsibility to look after his prized antiques. She stood in front of Moore twisting and turning her hands, inwardly fearing the loss of her position. Silence.

Then "No everything is fine Mrs. Stevens. I took them with me to London to be evaluated. I am sorry that I forgot to tell you." Together they went into the sitting room. Moore looked around. "Is that all that is missing?"

"Yes sir," Mrs. Stevens replied.

"And no strangers or tradesmen were in the house during the past two days?"

"Oh no Mr. Moore."

"Alright .Thank you Mrs Stevens."

The housekeeper quickly left as Moore continued to walk around the room. He was puzzled wondering why the thief had taken only four snuffboxes when there were twenty four in his collection. Besides the missing four, although valuable, were not the best. He went from room to room to confirm that nothing else was missing, even his Georgian silver tea service was still in its proper place and all his valuable paintings were still on the walls. He climbed the stairs still wondering, *"Why those and why just four?"*

Suddenly he felt violently sick, as if all his organs had seized up. His heart had stopped beating. He almost fell. Grabbing the stair rail for support he tried to run up the stairs but his legs would not budge. Taking deep breaths he managed to put one foot in front of the other and reach his bedroom. Nothing looked amiss but Moore instinctively felt something was badly wrong. With a still fluttering heart Moore went across to his dressing room. Nothing visibly amiss but that didn't stop his fingers trembling as he lifted down the painting and spun the lock on the wall safe. He now feared that the snuff boxes were just a red herring and that something much, much more valuable was the real object of the robbery. He took a deep breath and steadied himself as he swung open the safe door willing for the object to be there. When he saw the empty safe Moore knew the life that he had so carefully sculptured was over. Somebody knew who he was. Banging one fist into his other palm Moore yelled to his bedroom walls.

"Who would dare do this to me? I'll get them for this. When I'm finished with them they'll regret messing with me."

He was absolutely beside himself raging aloud shaking his fists and stomping across his bedroom. He'd never experienced so much anger, he had difficulty drawing a breath, momentarily he lost all control as a red mist clouded his sight and thunderous noises filled his ears. Then suddenly in a flash, his mind was filled with scenes of the most horrific acts of revenge he could meter out to whoever was responsible for this violation of his property. He heard a timid knock on his door.

"Are you alright Mr. Moore?" Mrs. Stevens called.

"Yes, yes I'm fine. Where are the children?'

"Down the village with Rosie," she answered.

"Very well, I will be down when they return." The knock on his door forced Moore to calm down. His breathing became more regular as he walked rather than stomped across the room.

"Think. Think I need to plan how to get my things back as quickly as possible."

The stolen package represented his life time's work and his family's future. He knew if it fell into the hands of the authorities then it would be a long prison sentence for him and his children would be left alone and penniless.

"Recovery is first and then I will arrange a slow, painful but decisive revenge on everyone involved." Moore recognized that whoever had committed this breach of the criminal's code was an expert; he also knew that it was more than a one man job. That, in Moore's estimation, was an advantage, he knew by experience that people talked and his men would soon get to hear something about last night's job. Breathing more evenly Moore opened his bedroom door, fully in control of himself, prepared to meet with his children as if all was well.

To the residents of the historic village Alex Moore was a widower with two young children, who owned the large red brick house situated in the shadow of the famous windmill. He was known as a man who jealously guarded his privacy with his house surrounded by a hedge so high it was impossible to see into the garden or the house unless one went through the front gate, or climbed up the hill to the Windmill and looked down. Moore employed local women to look after his family's needs and supported the village economy by purchasing goods from local shops. Often on a Saturday morning he strolled through the High Street making purchases and greeting the locals. He often dropped in at the local pubs for a friendly beer; he patronized the local arts and drama clubs and even accompanied his children to church on occasion. Physically Moore was a man who would not stand out in a crowd. Of average height and weight, clean shaven with dark hair and always dressed for the occasion even if some people thought his mannerism just a little effeminate. He was polite to everyone he met; he had a good memory for names and knew a little something about each of the more notable residents of the small village. He was respected as a contributing member of the small but, influential social group and his advice was often sought when the future of the village was under discussion. But Moore was nobody's fool for he was well aware that his carefully built respectability would come crashing down around his ears if he reported the burglary and the police started asking questions.

He ate his meal with his son and daughter and listened to their chatter and then explained that an emergency had arisen at one of his sites and he had to return to London for a few days.

"I'm truly sorry that I have to go away so soon." Moore said to his children, "I know we made some plans for a trip to Hastings tomorrow to listen to the band on the seafront but this is a real emergency. If you like I'll leave Rosie some money and she can take you on the bus somewhere for the day. Would you like that?"

"But you always take us out daddy" complained his daughter.

Moore leaned across the table and took her hand. "This is the first promise to you that I have broken and I am really sorry. I would much rather be with you two than go on back to dirty old London. But I'm must go and that is it."

"Alright, I suppose it's better than nothing, Can Rosie take us on the bus to Hastings?"

"Yes of course I will leave enough money for treats as well."

Quickly packing fresh clothes and taking certain items from a locked drawer he ran downstairs to his car. As usual Moore told Mrs. Stevens that should an emergency occur he would be either at his office or staying at his Knightsbridge club, but Moore also owned a luxurious flat in Mayfair and it was there that he was headed.

Growing up near the docklands in London life had been not been easy for the Higgins family, that being Moore's birth name. He remembered his father, a big, strong man with thick hairy arms and always dressed in work clothes. Mr. Higgins was a discontented man whose life revolved around two things, work and drink. Work was as frequent as the arrival of ships to be emptied or filled. Moore remembered days when his father would go off to work early in the morning and be home by breakfast time as the boat had been delayed out in the channel or more often Higgins had argued with the dock master who then refused him work for that day. That would result in a morning of shouting, swearing and hitting out at Moore's mother.

As soon as the pubs were open his father would be down there with his mates, he always had money for drink but very little for food or decent clothing for the five children he had sired. Mrs. Higgins was a frail, small woman who had simply given up on her husband. She did her best for the children and took in laundry from a couple of nearby boarding houses to put food on the table. She withstood both mental and physical abuse from her husband, telling the young ones that their father still loved them. Alex Higgins was the eldest of the five and had already learnt how to avoid his father's swinging blows and how to protect the smaller children during the nights when their father came home drunk.

There was little room in the mean, terraced house with privacy being completely foreign to the members of the Higgins family. The house had only two bedrooms upstairs, one for the parents and the baby, the other for the four older children. One ancient, large double bed with a straw mattress was all the children had. The staircase was narrow and dark with a door at the bottom that opened up directly into the back room. Even during the daytime the smaller children would huddle deep in the corner of the bend in the dark stairs believing that the darkness offered them some safety from their father's harsh words and heavy blows.

The lower floor of the house was equally small with two rooms and a scullery tacked on to the back. This is where Mrs. Higgins did all the laundry and young Higgins became all too familiar with the cloying atmosphere created by the steam from the continual boiling water and then the dank smell of damp laundry drying out. On a wet day the rain battered constantly on the tin roof of the kitchen and the laundry had to be dried in the living room in front of the black fireplace that served both as an oven and the place where all water was heated for the washing.

Often during the cold, damp winter days the younger children were unable to get close to the small fireplace as drying the washing was the economic necessity for Mrs. Higgins. If she couldn't get the neighbour's laundry dry on time then her opportunities to earn even a few shillings would be lost. So the children had to sit behind the washing and be satisfied with an occasional glimpse of the red flames. At least they did have some coal for the fire, but that was because Alex and his brother would follow the coalman's wagon down the street catching any odd bits of coal that fell off or flew out of the sacks as the full sacks were hoisted onto the coalman's shoulders for delivery. On Saturdays the boys hung around the market looking for free food. Quite often while their mother was paying for potatoes at the front of the stall the two Higgins boys would be at the back of the stalls looking for items that had fallen off, anything would do to help thicken their daily stew.

From the age of twelve Moore had plans to run away... He knew that somewhere out there, outside the dock area there were green places, where people lived safe and happy lives and that is what he wanted, that and tons of money. The accidental death of his brother had delayed his plans but when he was twelve Alex left school and was working for a man down at the market. It was this man who taught Moore the art of obtaining the unobtainable for a price. He watched and learnt how to buy cheap and sell dear. He grew close to those who always knew when a carton fell off the back of a lorry, or when a bale of goods disappeared from the dockside. He learned how to barter. He mixed with two kinds of people, the street-smart ones who could always sniff out a moneymaking deal and those who had the money to buy in.

By the time he was thirty Alex Higgins had his own flat, had re-invented himself as Mitchell, and was a wheeler-dealer in the black market trade. His father had abandoned the family, leaving on a merchant ship bound for Australia; his mother had simply died of despair. His younger sister was in service in a large house near Victoria station but he had no idea, or any interest, where the others were, for Mitchell, had no past. The present and making money had become his priority, his god. That was where his emotions went, making as much money as quickly as he could and if someone stood in his way, well too bad. Mitchell didn't give a damn about who he trampled over to add to his fortune.

When he was thirty-three Mitchell fell in love with a French girl who he met in a pub. For the first time in his life Mitchell cared for another person. They lived in a small, but genteel house in Kensington and had two children. Unfortunately Mitchell's happiness was short lived as his wife died three months after the birth of their second child, a daughter. Mitchell was devastated by her death. Even then, as a moderately wealthy man he was unable to prevent his wife's death and he vowed at her graveside to provide well for his children. His wife had never known where or how Mitchell made his money, as he was very careful never to show his wife his other side. But the loss of the one person who truly loved him rekindled the despair he felt as a boy. He was determined that somebody had to pay for his loss and the only way he knew to make real money was to go back to being the ruthless, hardnosed dealer of smuggled or stolen goods.

It was just a few years after his wife's death that Mitchell purchased the house in the small village and there built yet another personality, that of Mr. Moore, a kindly, community minded, respectable widower who had business interests in the City. Moore's rather dapper appearance belied the ruthless mind that lay behind the façade of a studied obsequisness. Many of Moore's business associates had lived, some had not, to rue the day they crossed paths with Alex Moore. His lonely and painful childhood had bred in him the understanding that it was always better to use others to get whatever he wanted. The ruthlessness that he had displayed in earlier years was nothing compared to the anger he directed to those who displeased him. That was the business Moore who resided in London. The outwardly gentler, considerate Alex who lovingly looked to the needs of his two young children, lived in the seaside village.

CHAPTER FIVE

Thomas Napier, alias The Leader, strode across Brighton station concourse to the Left Luggage Office where he exchanged a yellow ticket stub for a battered army duffel bag. Moving quickly he went down the tiled steps to the men's lavatories and re-emerged a few minutes later dressed exactly as the hundreds of businessmen who congested the station every weekday early morning. With his black suit, white shirt and dark blue tie, a bowler hat, a briefcase and the obligatory black umbrella Napier became one of the masses. Early mornings were hectic at the station, as hundreds of commuters crisscrossed the station concourse heading for their morning train to the City. Napier played this to his advantage and quickly merged into the throng of commuters striding across to Platform 5 and the fast train to Victoria. With black jackets flapping, black arms reaching up to secure bowler hats, umbrellas pointing the way and briefcases swaying to the rhythm of the black clad, ever moving legs, they moved forward like a flock of blackbirds preparing to take flight. The perpetual clatter of footsteps, the slamming of carriage doors, the continual low buzz of polite greetings, filled the station as passengers strove to reach their favourite seat before the guard blew his whistle.

Commuting to London each weekday had become a rite of passage for hundreds, men especially, as they clawed out a worthy position for themselves in that Mecca of British business, the City. Any stranger attempting to take an unoccupied seat would be subjected to glares, shaken newspapers and even the odd poke by an umbrella from those who objected to having their daily routine interfered with by some dreadful day-tripper person going to London.

Most of the carriages were labelled Third Class with the fewer First Class ones nearest the engine, purposefully giving the more well-heeled First Class passengers less distance to run when they disembarked at Victoria. With such a tradition Napier had to move several times before he secured a seat that wasn't already spoken for.

The houses and fields flew by but Napier had other concerns on his mind. He desperately wanted out of his current occupation. He was 30 years old and came from a respectable, hardworking family in the

Midlands. After attending the local grammar school and taking a few business courses at college he gained a position with a large London bank but a sudden downturn in the market and some poor investments had left the bank in some difficulty resulting in lost positions for its most junior clerks. Napier was understanding at first but as the weeks increased without any sign of a recall Napier decided to look for work down South.

His research had shown several financial opportunities listed in the local paper plus other junior management positions. He was well aware of Brighton's reputation of being the base for criminals, mostly of the lesser kind, but the town was also a thriving tourist destination for tens of thousands of Londoners who brought in tens of thousands of pounds in business each summer. With confidence Napier gave up his small London flat and headed down to the coast. He did have several positive interviews and was awaiting a letter regarding a position in Barclays when an opportunity of a different nature presented itself. Knowing that the position in the bank was a few weeks away and his finances were looking rather grim, he was eager to earn money on the side so when a drinking buddy mentioned that he and his mate were was looking for somebody to help out on a quick job Napier listened. When told that it was a night job and involved two other men Napier immediately knew this so-called work was questionable but the reality of his circumstances forced him to smother his indignant reaction and listen as his drinking buddy went through the details, guaranteeing there would be no violence. What broke Napier's resolve was the excessive amount of money that he would get for simply organizing a quick in and out burglary.

He was good and soon found himself being asked to organize more of these so called projects while inwardly cursing himself for being so successful. He wasn't a fool, he knew what he did was illegal, yet he felt he had no other choice as the bank continued to delay and finally fell through. He had been lucky so far, his name had never been connected to any crime and he had made good money. But he knew that soon his luck would run out and if he didn't make a break he would be trapped permanently on the wrong side of the law and likely spend several years in prison.

Last night's job had been ordered by a man known in the criminal fraternity as 'the Boss'. It was simple. Break into this posh house in Rottingdean, steal a leather wrapped package from the safe in the master bedroom and turn it over to him, the Boss, in London the next day.

As he looked out of the train window Napier remembered Rosie, the pretty young girl who went in twice a week to clean the house. He'd posed as a window cleaner and Rosie had been very helpful showing Napier all the windows that had to be cleaned and explaining her employer's usual schedule.

"You're new around here aren't you?" she'd asked when he told her why he was at the house.

"Yes, I'm just getting started in my own business. I was hoping that I could get some work on houses in the village."

"Well,' she said. "Mr. Moore doesn't like people around the house when he is here so if Mrs. Stevens lets you do the windows, you'd better come on a day when he is in London. Why don't you come in for a cup of tea and you can talk to Mrs. Stevens, she should be back from the shops by now."

But Napier was not keen to meet the housekeeper and had instead asked Rosie to have lunch with him the next day, her day off, down in the village.

"I'm not sure that I can do that, I don't know you."

"It will just be lunch," said Napier.

"Well you are clean and tidy and you talk nice. Alright then, I'll meet you at the café down by the greengrocers on the High Street about twelve-thirty."

Napier smiled to himself as he remembered the enjoyable hour he spent with Rosie. She was pretty and very talkative and innocently provided vital information for Napier over tea and a sandwich.

Napier always chose his partners carefully and though everything went as planned there was still something about the job that troubled him. Miller had performed well: no mess, no noise and had quickly disarmed the burglar alarm and opened the safe. Napier had no doubts that Miller was a survivor and would hold his tongue about last evening. But the young man? Bobby was a likeable young man typical teenager who amused Napier in the way he mimicked American postures like chewing gum and swaggering around in his colourful shirts. But the kid was a keen worker, did as he was told, never gave any lip and never asked questions. Last night the boy had done his job and had been especially skilled at managing the car in such bad weather, but this morning he seemed different, seemed anxious for Napier and Miller to get on their way. Bobby was always grinning, but this morning there was something more, a twinkle in the boy's eye implying that he knew something Napier didn't and that twinkle worried Napier.

Leaving the train Napier strolled outside to where numerous buses were waiting. He saw many travellers hurrying down the steps to the Underground while many more waited impatiently for the next empty taxi to arrive at the curb when they would open the car door, fling themselves into the back and be off without the vehicle coming to a stop. He would have a late breakfast at Lyons Corner House, one of his favourite eating places when he worked in London. There was plenty of time for the short bus ride to Piccadilly Circus, to have a leisurely breakfast, be on time for his meeting at Bishops Hotel and then be on the mid-afternoon train back home. He planned to catch the semi-fast back to Brighton, Miller would be waiting on the platform at East Croydon for his pay and Bobby would be hanging around Smith's at Brighton station. The agreed pay-out was very generous and Napier was determined to use his cut to begin a new life away from the South Coast.

The breakfast at Lyon's was as good as he remembered and evoked memories of the happier years he had spent in London. At the hotel he picked up a Daily Mail and then took a secluded seat in the lobby to wait for his contact. It was a seedy hotel, the furniture was shabby, the clerks' uniforms could do with a press and the people moving in and out did not give the appearance of being wealthy. But Napier was quite comfortable in these surrounding. Just as he turned to the Sports page he saw a tall, reedy looking man, wearing an old fashioned long, black overcoat and a wide brimmed black hat with a black scarf covering his lower face, stride up to the desk and ask loudly for the key to room 201.

Napier realized this was his contact. Was this strangely dressed man the mysterious Boss of whom nobody knew yet greatly feared, or another messenger? Napier had no idea who he was meeting. He had never actually met the Boss despite doing several jobs for him. Napier never concerned himself about the 'whys and wherefores' of a heist. He accepted the job order, hired the appropriately skilled individuals, organized and completed the job and then passed the goods to someone else, receiving the agreed payment in return. That was the end of his responsibility. He did not want to know any more.

Picking up the heavy briefcase Napier climbed the stairs to the second floor. The door of 201 was slightly ajar.

"Come in," called a gruff voice. Entering Napier was faced by the back of a very large wing-backed chair. All he could see of its occupant was the black hat, two black gloves and the back of black boots under the chair.

"Stay right there," the voice ordered. Then, "Any problems?"

"None," said Napier, still unable to see any features of the seated man. The man hooked one black, gloved hand over the arm of the chair and pointed to the table.

"Good. Put the case on the table, take the envelope and leave the hotel and the area immediately. And remember my warning." The man's tone of voice left no doubt in Napier's mind that this was a man not to double-cross.

Napier did as he was ordered, left the hotel quickly, hurrying around the corner to the bus stop. He was still tense from the meeting but still clambered to the top deck. It was always quieter upstairs. The Victoria bus had to pass back in front of the hotel and settling into his seat he glanced back. He did a double take as he saw a tall, thin man wearing a long black coat, hailing a taxi. Quickly Napier slid down further into his seat, praying that the man had not seen him.

As the bus wended its way through London Napier remembered the happier times living in the busy city with its diverse population, but today he had no wish to hang around. The London scene with its shops, its pageantry, and its theatres was exciting but now it left him cold, in a hurry to leave.

He was early for his return trip and took a seat beside the great clock and waited. The continual activity on Victoria Station was always entertaining. He watched, amused, at the antics of two station sweepers who appeared to be having words as they parked their dustcarts and headed towards the buffet, obviously on their tea break. One was wildly gesticulating as he mimicked a cricketer while the other kept nodding in agreement. Perhaps a comment on yesterday's match at the Oval wondered Napier. Then his attention was caught by a couple of youngsters dashing through the crowds, quickly glancing up at the departure board and then dashing off again.

"They left that a bit late," muttered the elderly man sitting beside Napier on the bench. Napier smiled in agreement. Then, out of the corner of his eye, he saw a movement he recognized. A long, flapping, black overcoat and the unusual hat were heading towards him.

"What the hell is he doing here" Napier muttered as he picked up his paper to cover his face forgetting, in his panic that he and The Boss had never met face to face. But the figure quickly disappeared down the stairs leading to the barbershop. Thankfully Napier saw that his train was in and almost ran across to the platform, greatly relieved to be on his way home.

CHAPTER SIX

His office door opened slowly, he heard Superintendent Young call out goodnight down the corridor and then he heard.

"Have time for a quick pint Jack?" The voice of his boss Detective Inspector Jones

"Yes sir. Just let me put this file away and I'll meet you at the door"

Together they strolled down past a few shops and swung into the corner pub, a favourite of both men. Like others around, the pub was a Georgian building dark with small windows. The old cobbled street was now bricked and led to the narrow streets of antique shops that made The Lanes of Brighton so famous.

"What will you have?" asked Smith, "A bitter or a Guinness?"

"No, put your money away," Jones told Sergeant Smith, "my treat today."

With only a few patrons in drinking, the pub was quiet and the officers were able to have a conversation without shouting. Smith was happily married with two teenage sons, whom Jones knew, were giving their parents a worrying time just now.

"How did Brian get on at the football last Saturday?" Jones asked.

"He did very well, scored a couple of goals and had a good game. I just wish he would put as much energy into his school work as he does into football," sighed Smith.

"Is he going to stay on at the Grammar School when he's written his exams?"

"No. he's determined that he's leaving to find some work that will take him through until he is eighteen and has to do his Service. Neither his mum or I can make him see that he is just wasting two years, We told him that he could get into an apprenticeship programme that would delay his call-up and provide him with a trade so that after he does his time he'll have something to build on. We've tried so hard to persuade him but he has stopped listening to us." Smith took a sip of his beer. "And then we have young Derek coming up who believes everything that Brian says and does is gospel."

"Can I help at all?" asked Jones.

"You and I both know that even now employment is still not where it was before the war and many former soldiers still haven't found suitable employment. Many wish there had been opportunities for apprenticeship before they had to go to war." Smith nodded his thanks and said that he would make the offer to Brian and see what he says.

"Changing the subject did you get that request for another CID car through to the Super"?

"Yes I did" replied Jones "But now it goes to the Chief Constable and as he is no friend of mine I can only hope that Supt. Young can persuade the man that we really need extra wheels."

"We certainly need another car, we also need more constables in CID. Every time the higher ups decide on a new policing model the paperwork doubles, the time spent filling them in doubles but the manpower stays the same. Instead of being out investigating the constables are tied down to their desks, Thank goodness we do have some civilian staff to help"

"Good day today though," said Jones, as the men got ready to leave.

"With only a few telephone calls to deal with I managed to get three reports out of the way."

Smith chuckled, "Well sir maybe all the criminals have gone on strike for a few days! But I wouldn't expect it to last." He called out as he turned away towards his car.

"We'll see tomorrow. Goodnight Jack," replied Jones as he headed towards the Pier for his walk along the Esplanade to his flat in Hove.

Jones loved to walk, he especially enjoyed walking along the seafront at high tide when the smells of saltwater and seaweed swirled around his face and up his nose. He found the experience bracing as it wiped away the mustiness of the age old building that presently housed the Sussex Police. He referred to his walks as his 'mobile think study" and used them not only to work through cases but also to generate new ideas, new lines on enquiry. But tonight his thoughts were focused on Jack Smith his wife Helen and their sons. …

I wonder what it is like to be responsible for two growing boys. It can't be easy, especially these days. I remember when my mother and grandmother would get so cross with me when I was a teenager. I don't think I was a bad lad but I missed dad and our trips together. I missed going to Cardiff to watch Wales play. I missed the Saturday morning climb up the mountain and then finding a spot to rest and eat our sandwiches. I used to marvel at granddad's knowledge of the village. He could point out just about where everybody lived and when we looked closely he could recognize the men working in their allotments just beside the canal. He knew the times of the buses and we would watch as the red Western Welsh bus would slowly wind its way through the village. Only one street mind you but lots of bends as it curled around the base of the opposite mountain We were all there back then, dad, granddad and we three boys.

In the days and months after the accident I remember being very angry at what had happened and refused to speak about it. I resented relatives and friends continually asking me how I felt. They should have known how I felt. I wanted to be left alone on my own private world where I pictured dad and granddad lying on the cold, hard surface of the coal seam, covered in fallen rocks and coal dust, not moving. I often wondered if they had died quickly or slowly waiting and praying to be rescued. Nobody knew as they were never recovered. I remembered thinking that the picture in my head was mine and only mine and if I spoke about it, it would never be mine again.

I find it hard to imagine how parents deal with angry children and certainly there's a great deal of anger about, after what the war did to us. Perhaps Jack's boys are as uncommunicative as I was. Nobody ever said that life was easy but the war created so many problems, even for us here, and we were supposed to be the victors! No wonder today's children have trouble seeing a future for themselves and become easily tempted to get into trouble.

CHAPTER SEVEN

It was a week after the Rottingdean job and young Bobby Williams was impatient to get some more money. The payoff for the job was good but by the time he had paid his housekeeping to his mother, bought a few records and the tickets for the soccer match, there wasn't as much left as he had hoped. He'd hung around the house reading his dad's paper hoping to see the robbery mentioned. He'd even read the Herald down at the Fish and Chip shop, but still nothing. He was puzzled. He knew whatever was taken from upstairs at the house was very valuable. After all nobody would show or tell him what it was but still Bobby was flattered to be involved in such an important heist. To him it was the first step up the criminal ladder and when word of his reliability and driving skills was spread he knew he would have plenty of work lined up. But now he was frustrated, Bobby wanted good things to happen quickly and he couldn't understand why his plans were being thwarted. He banged his fist on the kitchen table.

"What's up Bobby?"

"Oh nothing Mum. Just wanted to read about summat and it aint here."

Waving her mixing spoon at him she called, "Well just you make sure you fold your dad's paper up properly or you know they'll be hell to pay when he gets home."

"Okay mum. I'm going round to see Bert; he should be home now he's on the early shift. See ya."

"Don't be late for dinner," she called after him just as the door slammed.

His parents, well his dad mostly, had been nagging him to get out and find some regular work, but that did not interest Bobby. He was not going the way of some of his schoolmates. He saw them riding their bikes back and forth to work every day just for a couple of quid a week. Oh, he told his dad that he went down to the Labour Exchange but there was never anything for him. No, he had other plans. Living in London and mixing with the 'big boys' was his ambition.

Bobby believed implicitly that life was full of opportunities if you had the guts to become a player. He viewed Rottingdean as a first step towards independence and impatiently waited for the next job. But he had to solve another problem. This weekend his favourite soccer team was playing at home and Bobby was determined that he would take his three mates up to London in style, and for Bobby that meant getting another car now that his old Hillman was gone. And of course he had to have new gear to go with his new wheels.

Clothes and cars were essential for Bobby's self-esteem but they cost more money than Bobby could lay his hands on. He could never ask his parents for a loan, his dad did not earn much and besides Bobby there were three younger children to feed and clothe. Bobby knew he was on his own and if the trip to London was to happen then more money had to be found.

He had saved some of his pay from the job which he added to his growing stash from earlier jobs but Bobby determinedly kept hold of that in readiness for moving to London. No, the money for this weekend had to be found elsewhere.

He walked down to Bert's house working out his frustration by kicking at the few pebbles that were up on the pavement and muttering to himself.

"Oh Christ, what am I going to do, It's too soon, but I already got the tickets for Saturday's game. And I promised the boys. I aint got much choice do I?"

He and Bert spent that evening together playing darts at their local, although underage they had their customary couple of beers, then wandered off to go home.

"What's the matter with you then Bobby?" asked Bert.

"Why, what do yer mean?"

"Well you seem to be off somewhere else tonight. We could 'ave beat those two idiots at darts but you kept missing your shots. What's up then?"

"I'm thinking about Saturday, all the arrangements. Gotta get a car and think of somewhere to stay."

"Why where's yours then?" asked Bert. Bobby realized his mistake and quickly added. "Oh flat tyres."

"Can't we go by train then?" suggested his friend.

"No. I promised you lot a special trip and besides the others don't have the money for the fare."

"Okay. See you tomorrow, we'll work somefink out," called Bert turning into his front gate.

Bobby didn't answer him, he was still thinking about getting wheels for Saturday. He had worked a few of the lesser robberies in the Brighton area and learned the names of a couple of antique dealers who were not too fussy about where items came from.

"Shouldn't be too 'ard to sell them," he said out loud and with the unshakeable confidence of youth Bobby knew that the time had come for him to become an independent trader.

Bobby knew exactly where each of the shops were located in The Lanes. He was going to be cautious but cool. Walking through the old narrow streets, he pretended to be a casual visitor, just one of the thousands of tourists who visit the historic streets every year looking for bargain antiquities. With his hands in his pockets he sauntered along the cobbled pavement stopping to study the front window of each small shop. Soon he reached the first of his targets. Still affecting a nonchalant manner he studied the window display, but this time he was looking to see if the owner was inside. Casually, Bobby entered the shop involuntarily jumping as the doorbell clanged to announce his arrival. The man was seated at a desk hunched over a very large magnifying glass. He looked up as Bobby entered.

"Morning," said Bobby. The man never said a word, just peered at Bobby over the top of his glasses.

The shop consisted of long glass-topped counters running the full length on each side of the shop with taller glass fronted cabinets against the two walls. Bobby started at the counter just by the door and walked slowly along pretending an interest in everything he saw. Finally he spotted a case that held several snuffboxes. Still trying for nonchalance Bobby asked,

"What yer want for this one then?" He didn't move to look at the owner as he was concentrating on leaning against the wooden base of the counter to stop his knees trembling as well as trying his best not to cough in the smoky atmosphere.

"Fifty quid," was the curt reply.

Bobby carried on looking while fingering the two items in his pocket and wondering what he should do next. He had no idea of the real value of his items, after all he wasn't a jeweller, but he knew enough to know that they were very old, perhaps Georgian, and were marked 'Sterling Silver'. As he walked up and down looking in the display cases and still fiddling in his pockets Bobby realized that the dealer was watching him just a bit too closely for comfort. Bobby was unaware that there had been several 'snatch and grab' robberies in the Lanes during the past week. But the dealer knew and was beginning to have suspicions that this rather shabbily dressed young man was part of that gang.

"Well do you want it or not?" snapped the dealer, moving towards the door ready to throw Bobby out.

"No, not just now, I'll fink about it, thanks mate," Bobby quickly made his escape into the street.

"Blimey," said Bobby to himself "this ain't going to be so easy".

He turned right at the church, down Meeting House Lane to find a café whose owner he knew well. Bobby ordered a fried egg sandwich and then asked Brian if he had a decent overcoat and a tie he could borrow for an hour. He took the clothes into the lavatory and set about making himself look more creditable. He washed his hands and face, slicked down his hair with water, used a wet rag to clean off his shoes and dust off his trouser bottoms. Bobby was blessed with an honest face and his cheeky grin helped smooth his way through his young life. He was not a cruel or vindictive young man, he loved and respected his parents but he was determined that his life would be different.

By the time he'd put on Brian's tie and coat he was satisfied with his new look.

Next, using a lower more mature tone, he practiced in the mirror what he would say to the next dealer.

Satisfied he left the cafe and headed back down Meeting House Lane until he reached the shop of the second dealer. Again he looked in the shop's small window. Bobby could see a young lady assistant at the counter but taking a deep breath he boldly opened the door and stepped into the shop. The girl looked up as the inside bell clattered.

"Is the manager in? I wish to speak to him," Bobby politely asked, in his newly adopted grammar school accent.

"Mr. Sinclair is in the back room, can I help you sir?" Bobby was momentarily speechless. Nobody had ever called him Sir before.

Regaining his poise he confidently replied,

"Thank you but I have valuable items to sell and I insist on dealing with Mr. Sinclair."

As the assistant went away to fetch her boss Bobby inhaled deeply, he felt confident but he knew he was dealing with someone well known in the business and that knowledge made it difficult to breathe evenly. Stepping from behind a purple, velour curtain a short, stout, older man moved into the shop's light. He was wearing tortoiseshell glasses with thick, double glass lenses that made his eyes look like those of a codfish. He had sandy coloured hair, which was combed backwards.

"Probably a comb over," muttered Bobby under his breath but he also knew that this man was the dealer he was looking for. Mr. Sandy Sinclair.

"Can I help you?" he politely asked Bobby.

Maintaining his plumy accent Bobby replied sharply,

"You certainly can. My grandfather recently passed on and the old chap left me some small pieces of silver. I will keep the majority of pieces but I want to sell these two snuffboxes."

Sinclair looked at both boxes and then taking a small magnifying glass out of his waistcoat pocket he examined every surface and every corner of each box. Each time he turned the box over he would peer over the top of his glasses at Bobby.

"Where did you say you got these?" he asked again, looking straight at Bobby.

"From my grandfather's estate. He lived in a big house in Kent, near Faversham."

To Bobby's relief the dealer did seem very interested but Bobby wished that he would stop looking at him, stop asking questions and make an offer.

"What will you give me for them?" asked Bobby attempting to speed things up, he suddenly had this feeling that he needed to get away, far, far away from this shop.

"Twenty quid a piece," offered the dealer.

"Not enough for good pieces like this," insisted Bobby. "I need at least fifty pounds for each or I will take them elsewhere."

After more wrangling they settled on forty-five pounds for each box.

As he waited for Sinclair to complete his paperwork Bobby wandered around, looking in the display cases and fingering some of the items on the counter

Sinclair reappeared from behind the curtain.

"At last," thought Bobby and tapped his foot against the counter as Sinclair separately counted out each note

"Where's my receipt?" asked Bobby but Sinclair ignored his question and walked quickly around the counter to open the door for Bobby.

"Well?" Bobby held out his hand.

"Don't push your luck young man. Just go." Bobby realized he had been found out and almost leapt out of the shop door, very aware of Sinclair's eyes boring into his back.

Outside he quickly left for the Old Steine area and the buses. He was desperate to put some distance between himself and The Lanes and he didn't feel safe until he was on the bus home. Even then he sat on the upper deck, as he wanted to make sure no one was following him. He took a deep breath. All went well but his first adventure into the world of illegal fencing was very frightening, but the crisp feel of the new banknotes in his pocket made it all worthwhile. Now, finally he had enough money for the weekend in London. He had already picked out the car, promising to pay the deposit that evening. Saturday they were off to watch the best match of the season. A London derby where he just knew that his idols Arsenal, would give Chelsea the hammering of their lives.

As soon as Bobby left his shop Sinclair hurried into the backroom to check his accounts book. He had recognized the snuffboxes immediately and knowing who the owner was, he knew that unless he was very careful he would be involved in a very nasty happening. Running his fingers down the listings he came to the entry he sought; he was holding his breath hoping that he was wrong. No, he had sold each of the boxes to Mr. Moore. They were two of a set of four he had sold about two years ago.

He shut his accounts book slowly, quietly, wanting to delay the inevitable. He had often dealt with Moore, selling him jewellery and antiques from legitimate sellers but Sinclair had also sold the man items that were not so legit. The only connection he and Moore had was in antiques but through other sources Sinclair knew that Moore was ruthless. Sinclair knew that Moore's business was trading goods; he also knew that nobody ever questioned where the goods came from. Word on the street was that a couple of consignment jobs for Moore had gone sour and the people involved paid dearly for their mistakes.

Sinclair had immediately recognized the snuffboxes when Bobby pulled then out of his pocket. Never believing, for an instant, Bobby's story or his accent, Sinclair knew the boxes had been stolen from Moore. Although there was no word of a robbery, either through his grapevine or in the newspapers Sinclair knew what he had to do. Taking a deep breath he called Moore's telephone number. Mrs. Stevens answered and told Sinclair that Mr. Moore had gone up to London for a couple of days. Sinclair had a London number for him so once again he dialled a number. The man answering agreed to take a message and took down Sinclair's name and telephone number stating that Mr. Moore would be back in the late afternoon.

Exceedingly upset at finding himself in this position Sinclair sat shuffling papers around on his desk trying to calm himself down. At times Sinclair had wondered if Moore was actually the so called Boss but now he knew he was wrong. Who would dare rob the Boss in his own house? Sinclair called to his assistant.

"Sheila, I have to go out for a few minutes. Look after the shop please."

Pulling his raincoat over his shoulders, slipping on his black beret he practically ran out of his shop.

It was just one o'clock and he headed for the pub around the corner for a quick pint to steady his nerves. Sitting in the shadows at the corner table, first gulping and then sipping his pint Sinclair took stock of what had happened. He knew that Moore would want a description of the young man and his name, which unfortunately Sinclair did not know. All he knew was that he had seen the kid a couple of times at the racetrack hanging around with the bookies. That's all he knew. Moore would not be satisfied with so little information and Sinclair knew he would be forced to meet up with one of Moore's thugs who would be bound to pay him a visit,

There was one familiar person sitting up at the bar.

"Come and have a drink with me," invited Sinclair as he ordered two pints.

"How's things?" Sinclair asked when Al was seated at the corner table.

"Not bad Sandy, not bad at all. I won a few quid on the geegees last week an' I've bin clearing out some old houses for the auctioneer, so not bad at all," said Al, slurping away at his pint of ale.

"How's the family, kids growing up now?"

"Yea, eldest is seventeen working in the dairy and youngest, young Al, is still at school, the missus is still 'doing' for the lady up on Dyke Road. How about you Sandy, life treating you alright?"

"Can't complain," was the reply. But then Sinclair bent down closer to Al and whispered to him.

"No. I ain't heard nuffink about one this month, whose house got hit?" was Al's response to Sinclair's whisper.

"Can't tell you that, not safe."

Sinclair quickly finished up his beer, nodded goodbye to Al and headed back to his shop. On the way back Sinclair decided that at the earliest opportunity he would leave Sheila in charge of the shop and he would disappear until this matter blew over.

Sheila was humming away to herself as she vigorously polished some silver desert spoons. Hanging up his coat Sinclair casually asked her if she had ever seen the young man who brought in the snuffboxes.

"Not in here Mr. Sinclair but I have seen him waiting for the bus over on North Street. He's usually with a crowd of his mates. Real loud ones those, always making such a noise," she screwed up her face in disapproval. "Most of them usually got on the bus up to the Elm Grove," she added.

Sinclair was very relieved; at least he could pass on one more bit of information to Moore. Sinclair knew that when the young man was tracked down he would be in a lot of trouble. Sinclair did not believe in violence and was troubled by what he had to do, but it was him or the boy so he felt he really had no choice.

Just then the telephone rang Sinclair moved behind the velour curtain to take the call.

"Is that you Sinclair?" asked the stern voice at the other end.

"Yes Mr. Moore."

"Well what do you have for me?"

"I had a young chap come in today offering two snuffboxes for sale. I knew that they were yours because I had them recorded in my Sales book. I wondered how he had got hold of them. Did you have a robbery Mr. Moore?"

There was silence from the other end. Sinclair wondered if he had asked one question too many. But Moore made light of it saying,

"The window cleaner's boy went to the lavatory inside and he must have lifted them. I hadn't even noticed they were gone."

"Well I bought the boxes from him and I have them here in the shop for you." Sinclair had to offer the snuffboxes but knew that he would not get his money back. He didn't care about that all he wanted was to be out of this situation.

"Did you know the boy?" asked Moore.

"Not by name, but I have seen him around the racetrack and places." answered Sinclair truthfully.

"Any idea where he lives?"

"No, but my assistant has seen him catching the Elm Grove bus here in North Street. Why don't you check with the window cleaner?" There was silence from the other end then,

"I'll send somebody down Monday afternoon, be ready." Then more silence down the telephone and then the line was cut.

Sinclair put down the 'phone. He was sweating, he had done all he could and even offered the snuffboxes back free, but he knew that it would not end there. Moore had been calm and rational but calmness in Moore did not necessarily mean he was satisfied or that it was the end of the matter. No, now that Moore was concerned enough to send somebody from London down to check out the situation Sinclair knew that he would be dragged even deeper into this mess. He was a very troubled man by the time he closed his shop that evening.

CHAPTER EIGHT

Moore went into the lounge of the exclusive London club and ordered a double whiskey from the waiter. He needed to think about his next step. He now had some information about one member of the gang of thieves but he felt sure that a kid could not have planned and carried out such a daring raid on his property. No, he had to look for more gang members but having a partial description of one would, given time, lead to the others.

But why only two boxes, where were the other two and where was his cache of jewellery? Who organized the raid on his house? Certainly not the kid. Moore was very well informed on the criminal activities along the south coast and could name most of criminals by names based on their patterns of crimes but even he was at a loss to think who could have pulled off this one. But he would have him whoever he was.

Finishing his whiskey Moore left his club and walked to his own flat. It was there that he kept all his 'other' business papers and records. It was there that he had hidden away, in one of his First Editions, the names and addresses of those people who could provide solutions to his problems. Although the list was not long the names included enforcers, collectors and dealers, specialized thieves, fences, a harbour master and even an Excise officer. Although very anxious to get his jewellery back Moore knew that he had to move secretively to discover the identity of first the gang members and then the organizer.

He couldn't move on a weekend as Brighton was always full of hundreds of shoppers, the buses were crowded as hundreds more headed for the seafront. A dangerous time to send in his team. Too many watching eyes about. Moore also knew that Sunday was out. Lately the Brighton police had increased their patrols both at the railway station and down West Street watching for London crooks trying to come in to Brighton as day-trippers. Moore knew of several lesser crooks who had been picked up on arrival at Brighton station. So Moore decided to hold off sending his men down to Brighton. In fact he knew that picking up the kid would be much easier after the weekend as the boy would think that he got away with it and would be more relaxed and back in his old haunts.

The large man watched intently out of the train window. Although the train had already stopped at several busy stations he was alone in his compartment. Twice people had wrenched the door open to climb in, looked up, saw him and hurriedly changed their minds, quickly walking on to another compartment. He didn't care. He knew that his large frame, staring eyes and scarred face frightened people but it didn't bother him, after all he wouldn't be good at his business if he looked like an angel.

He'd finished with the newspaper having read all the weekend soccer results and commentaries but he needed to keep carrying the paper, open at the Sports page, when he met his contact in Brighton. World news or politics were of little interest, just the sports and cartoons for him. Boarding the semi-fast train at Victoria he'd settled in for the hour and half journey south to Brighton. Mr. Moore had stipulated that the situation had to be resolved that day and that he would meet them at the designated spot around 8.30 that evening.

He was very familiar with the streets of Brighton and while stopping briefly to pick up cigarettes while continually checking for police it didn't take him long to reach Sinclair's shop.

Some antique shops were closed, depending on weekend business to make sales, but Sandy Sinclair was open every days. Sandy had never married and his only relative was an aged aunt who lived somewhere down near Southampton. He told Sheila, his assistant, that his aunt lived in one of those genteel residential hotels, which were so popular with older people. Sandy was devoted to his business. Each day he would follow the same routine of catching the number 52 bus down from his home in Hove and spend all day just pottering about in the shop.

This afternoon Sheila had left for a visit to her dentist and as things were relatively quiet Sinclair absently fiddled around in his shop, pretending to be doing inventory but knowing that soon he would have company. A very unwelcome guest as far as Sinclair was concerned.

The large man strode Sinclair's shop placing the open newspaper on the counter at the Sports Page, and nodded at Sinclair saying said he was an associate of Mr. Moore. Sinclair had no doubt that this huge man, who almost filled his shop was Moore's thug and readily gave him all the information he could about young Bobby. Then, disguising himself with a cap and scarf, Sinclair took the big man in a circular route around the small, narrow streets until they came out opposite but just above, the bus stop. They would wait until the boy showed up and then the man from London would follow him. But Sinclair was very agitated,

"What if he doesn't come today? What if he's working? Or run away?" he asked. Sinclair hands were clenched into tight fists and were pushed deep into his pockets almost pushing through the lining. The big man just shrugged.

"Mr. Moore was sure that a cocky little beggar like him would think he'd got away with it and would be doing his usual thing. So don't worry 'e'll show."

Sinclair hated this hanging about and continually paced to and fro around the corner and back again. He was desperate that none of his neighbouring shopkeepers would see him in the company of this thuggish character. But he also knew that the Clock Tower area was a mecca for teenagers. The record shops, cheap clothing stores and cafés drew in hundreds of kids every day.

Sinclair could see a group of teenagers noisily making their way through the crowded pavement towards the bus stop. Sinclair edged back into the shadow of the Barclay's Bank entrance, hiding yet able to see as the shouting, laughing group of young people grew closer. The big man stayed on the pavement and watched as the noisy group passed by. Looking back at Sinclair he raised his eyebrows... Sinclair pulled down his scarf and muttered, "Yes he's wearing the Arsenal scarf. Not the tall thin one but the shorter boy with the flash cap."

Sinclair hurried back around the corner, he was terrified didn't want anything more to do with this. He didn't want to watch the big man get on the bus for he knew that the boy would be lucky to survive the night and that he, Sinclair would be held as responsible as if he did the beating. He wanted to get home as soon as possible. In fact, he had decided to close up the shop and on his shop he hurriedly wrote a note for Sheila explaining that his aunt, in Southampton, was ill and he would be away for at least a week. He asked Sheila to keep the shop closed until Wednesday and then she could reopen. He would pay her for the missed work. Sinclair taped the note to the shop door and closed up.

Sinclair liked Sheila. She was just a slip of a girl who liked to go dancing at the Regent and would talk about nothing but boys and clothes should he let her. But she was intelligent and spoke nicely to the customers and was quickly learning the trade, so he was very happy with her and didn't want her involved in this mess.

Bobby was at the bus stop, clowning around with some other young people who, like him could never seem to stand still for more than a few seconds. They never queued up like the adults; they just stood there playfully pushing each other around until the bus pulled up. But they did wait their turn to get on, then yelled a boisterous "See ya" to their friends who were waiting for the next bus and then scrambled up the metal spiral stairs clattering all the way down to the front seats. There were four of them spread across the four double seats keeping up a continuous babble of conversation as they made themselves comfortable. The others passengers, behind them just looked at each other and raised their eyebrows, most of them knew the boys and were used to their noise and as long as the boys didn't swear or spit they left them alone.

The big man had also gone upstairs after the boys but had taken a seat at the back where he knew he would still be able to hear their conversation. People turned to look at him for they knew the regular bus passengers and he was a stranger. They waited to see what would happen when the man who regularly sat in the back seat got on at the Level stop but after taking one look at the stranger occupying his usual seat the new passenger quickly decided to sit elsewhere. As the bus continued along Lewes Road and turned up the Elm Grove the majority of passengers gradually left. Halfway up the Grove two of the boys called out.

"See ya later," as they ran down the stairs and hopped off at the next stop. Then Bobby and Bert left their seats ready to get off at the following stop. They were halfway down the stairs when Bobby turned saying, "Dirty Duck Bert, 8.00 o'clock sharp don't forget."

"Righto Bobby. As if I would. Looking forward to the match."

The man from London followed the boys and purposefully overtook them as they ambled down the street. He knew exactly where that pub was, it was called the Black Swan as he knew from previous visits on Race Days. Now he had to walk up the short way to the parking lot at the Race track, find his colleague and make plans to snatch Bobby.

Watching for Bobby was easy. After a quick look inside the pub to see if Bobby had arrived early two men parked the van just around the corner and sat in the semi darkness until they spotted the young man ambling his way down the street. It was a gloomy evening and as most of the patrons of the pub were already inside lifting their glasses nobody was there to watch as Bobby was stopped and spoken to by the driver of the van. Bobby wasn't a fool but he was flattered when the man spoke about a prospective job and wanted Bobby in on it. Bobby willingly climbed into the van as all thoughts of the darts match faded at the thought of him being recognized as a player in the big game.

"Get in. We'll discuss details in the van," the large man whispered.

As he saw Bert coming down the road he lifted his two thumbs as a salute. Bobby knew this wouldn't take long and he would soon be back to take part in the darts match. He thought it strange when the van suddenly took off down the street but the big man explained that they had to meet the last member of the team to "Complete the planning for the job" were his exact words.

Moore was waiting for them in a decrepit old stable that belonged to an abandoned horse farm on the west side of the Racehill. When he saw Moore in his smart suit and real leather shoes Bobby thought that here was a real criminal and that the job must be a big one. But the man was not friendly and it didn't take Bobby long to realize that he had been tricked and that he was in deep trouble.

"Hey. What's this all about then?" he shouted, struggling as he was pulled out of the van and pushed into the musty building. The two enforcers began their persuasive technique by pounding Bobby with their fists, while shouting at him to tell what he knew about the Rottingdean job. In vain Bobby tried to get away but the large man held him fast against the wall. Grunting with each swing the blows came faster and more powerful .When Bobby cried out.

"What yer want? I only took the boxes, nuffink else." Then things got uglier. Out came the knuckledusters and chains. Each time the assailants stopped for breath Moore, who was hidden in the shadows, asked Bobby questions about the robbery. Bobby admitted that he was the driver and that he had taken the snuffboxes but denied over and over again that he had gone upstairs.

"No, it was them other two, they did upstairs, I had to wait in the kitchen for them."

"No. I didn't see what they got," screamed Bobby, trying to avoid another blow. The big man had found a thick chunk of wood and the blows continued to rain down on the boy as each man took turns hitting him with the chain or the block of wood. They went after his legs and his arms the smaller one deliberately trod on Bobby's fingers breaking two at the first knuckle. By now Bobby had crumbled into the corner, his hands covering his bloody face. He was sobbing and mumbling and begging them to believe that he knew nothing about the planning of the job, that he was only a kid who did the driving. He had told Moore that one of the thieves was a safecracker, a small wiry man, from somewhere outside of London. He knew nothing about the other one only that he wasn't the Boss because he had to deliver the goods in London the next morning.

"Who was he going to see?" demanded the voice from the shadows.

"Honest, I don't know nuffink about the others, I was just the driver. Let me go I won't tell nobody," sobbed Bobby. They had punched and kicked him mercilessly over his head and chest and now he was making strangling sounds as he tried to regain his breath.

"Get him out of here;" ordered Moore, "he's finished. That'll teach him to mess with me." As the two thugs began pulling Bobby to his feet he made a small coughing sound, his eyes fluttered and he collapsed in their arms. He wasn't breathing at all; blood was coming out of his nose and his right ear.

"The little bugger is dead," they said, in unison.

"So. Too bad. Get rid of it somewhere on a building site or something and get the hell out of here."

Moore waved his arms at them impatiently, implying that he was not concerned any more. They dragged the body out of the barn, piling it into the back of the black van and sped away down the hill towards

Lewes Road. Anxious to get rid of their dead passenger they searched for a suitable dumping spot.

Just beyond The Level they spotted an open building site a little way down Baker Street. Hastily turning the lights off, the driver slowly bought the van to a stop. They both looked around, slid out of the front seats and working their way behind the vehicle opened the back doors and quickly carried the body a little way into the site. Bobby was not much of a weight and the large man had no trouble tossing him over his shoulder like an old worn out carpet. Keeping a watchful eye for nosy neighbours they spent a few minutes covering the body with bricks and rubble before returning to the van and driving slowly away from the curb. Traffic was light and soon they were headed back to Brighton station.

Dropping off the big man near the main railway station the driver made his way back to Clermont Terrace. Leaving the van exactly where he'd picked it up that morning; he put on the railway uniform, picked up the bag and flags and headed back along the road into Preston Park station just in time to catch the last semi-fast train to London.

While his two enforcers were making their way back to London, Moore had walked across the few hundred yards to his car parked well away from the old horse barn. It was now ten o'clock on an especially dark night. It was always dark up on the Racehill as the track sat just outside the residential rim of Brighton. A wide-open area where streetlights were non-existent and night traffic seldom ventured. Every hour there was a bus, but Moore knew that he would be long gone before the next one came rumbling up the hill. He was sure anyone who passed his car would be certain to think that it belonged to a courting couple hidden in the fields behind the bushes. A grassy area notorious for illicit meetings.

Back at his house Moore drove the car into an old shed at the end of a piece of wasteland behind his property. The first thing he did was to check the wheels for mud and grass. Once he was satisfied that they were clean he quickly closed and bolted the shed door then walked swiftly down the hidden laneway to his backdoor. Moore had used a car that was seldom out on the road and although properly registered it was not his name on the ownership disc.

Settling down behind his large, oak desk Moore reflected on the evening events. He had not learned as much as he had hoped although the boy had admitted to taking two snuffboxes. Obviously the boy knew very little about either his partners or the organizer behind the job. But Moore also recognized that had the boy not decided to steal the snuffboxes he would still be totally in the dark about who had entered his home. He held no regrets about Bobby's death it was just bad luck for the kid. You win some you lose some, was Moore's philosophy although Moore never liked to lose at anything and somebody always had to pay for Moore's losses.

He began to list what he did know; that there were two others in his house, the safecracker was an expert and the leader was considered reliable enough to be trusted to take the proceeds back to London.

Moore's network of informers was spread across the Home Counties. He didn't operate very often north of London as his business dealings needed ports, railways and ferries that were in abundance along the south coast, as were the majority of his rich and affluent customers. Moore knew that he would have to return to London the next morning and put his network to work searching out the other two thieves. He switched off the light and went upstairs, checked on his children and fell asleep without a moment's remorse about the killing of young Bobby Williams.

CHAPTER NINE

It was getting dark. The boys knew they would have to go in soon for tea.

"Come on Col. let's do one more run up over the bricks, down past the broken bathtub and over the wall." That was Jimmy, the eldest of the two brothers, always wanting to get the very most out of their free time. Although they had been told a dozen times not to go near the building site it was their favourite place to play and a wonderful place to find little treasures for their collections. Jimmy was ahead scrambling up the uneven bricks with Colin not too far behind. Suddenly both boys yelled as the pile of bricks began to slide backwards. The boys fell down scraping their knees on the rough edges of the rubble.

"What happened?" yelled Jimmy.

"I dunno," answered Colin as he sat one hand rubbing the scrapes on his knees and the other brushing away tears of pain. They were both looking at the bricks to see what has caused them to fall when Colin let out loud yell.

"What's that there?" pointing to something protruding from the bricks. Jimmy pushed his little brother out of the way and very cautiously started to pull away some of the other rubble. But even he jumped back when he saw that it was a human hand.

"Oh gawd," screamed Jimmy and grabbing Colin by the arm dragged him across the rubble. It was rough and the boys fell down in their hurry to get away from that thing. They hurled themselves down the road shouting "Mum, Mum, come quick." A small woman stepped out of one of the brightly coloured doors,

"What is it now I'm busy getting your father's tea?"

They pumped her hands and pulled her further on to the street still shouting at her to come and see what they'd found. She could see that her boys were really scared so she gathered them both up into her arms and calmly said, "Come in and tell your dad, he'll know what to do," and pushed them into the house.

A minute later both boys and a man left the house rushing up the street to the site. The father wasn't really sure what his boys had been up to but he had to look. Clambering over the rubble, cursing at the bricks as they dug into his legs, he reached where his boys pointed.

"There dad, just there," yelled Jimmy who was anxious to go closer but was frightened. Realizing that there was probably an entire body under the bricks Mr. Ames immediately sent Jimmy off to the local police reporting box, to tell P.C. Stock, while gently moving Colin back to the pavement. Within minutes Jimmy was running back down the road vainly trying to keep up as P.C. Stock furiously pedalled his bicycle down the street.

"I called it in," said the constable, panting from his exertion, "they should be along soon."

Meanwhile a crowd had gathered near Mr. Ames, all eager to see what was going on. Just as Constable Stock was removing the last of the bricks covering the body a police car came screaming around the corner stopping suddenly alongside the crowd. Immediately, two men jumped out and ordered Stock to tell the crowd to move back.

The policemen went to speak to Mr. Ames and then moved across to look at the body. They each circled the body, making notes and then bending down studying the face and then the clothes. Suddenly one policeman ran back to the car and spoke into the car 'phone. The buzz of the onlookers grew louder as they began to question each other what was happening. The ambulance had arrived but the attendants had not moved from their vehicle.

"Looks like they're waiting for someone else to come and look," said one.

"Yea," agreed his colleague and they placed the stretcher back in the ambulance. Lit their cigarettes and leant against the back door until they were needed.

Jones had been working on a report for his superintendent regarding the increased number of smuggling activities being carried out along the South coast. Scotland Yard had determined that most of the goods, mostly drugs but also small amounts of diamonds, were being transferred from small private boats coming across the Channel from Europe and docking at local ports or private marinas which were dotted all along the coast.

The Yard had created a national network of local detectives, dockyard police and Custom and Excise officers from each of the counties affected by these activities. The object being to share information and resources and bring this trade to an end. While stationed at Liverpool Jones investigated several cases of contraband goods being smuggled into the country via Liverpool Docks. It had been a long grinding investigation that took him across the Channel to make important contacts at European ports. His small team had been successful in bringing to justice some of the gangs involved in smuggling drugs and several of the bosses were now safely locked away for a long time. This experience meant that Jones became a pivotal man in this new network, at heart he was a strategist who believed that with clearly defined goals, a good communication system between members and the availability of needed resources he could make any plan work. He knew from experience that each force involved had to have the full support of its senior administration ready to provide the personal and financial resources to make this plan effective and enforceable.

He was excited at being such an integral part of such a widespread network of police departments and even more flattered when asked to be the lead officer. He looked forward to the collegiality that emerged when working with officers from around the counties as well as those from the Yard. As project leader he also knew that it would be up to him to keep both the information flowing and the momentum going. But he was also well aware that they would be officers who were not so cooperative, either due to territorial issues or just plain jealousy, but Jones was experienced in dealing with people who found change difficult, he referred to them as 'blockers' and in his past experience working with large diverse groups he had been forced to develop strategies to circumvent any blocks and tolerate the sceptics.

When first approached about the high jacking concerns Jones was determined that this criminal activity would not be allowed to increase on his patch. He knew that smuggling, whether it was petty pilfering or large-scale operations, attracted the most violent of criminals.

In the meantime Sgt Smith had been clearing up a few outstanding reports on a variety of misdemeanours by a gang of local lads. These boys enjoyed nothing more than going around the London Road shopping area throwing bricks into shop windows. Nothing was ever stolen, it was done simply for the thrill of it. But one of the gang was caught red-handed by a vigilant beat P.C. and it wasn't long before the police had all the names and the boys and their parents had been bought to the station. Smith had assigned P.C. Masters the job of organizing the interviews but some of the parents were very angry and turned on the young detective as he tried to establish names, addresses, ages and all the other details needed for his report. The parents had shouted at him accusing him of deliberately picking on their children just because they happened to be in the vicinity of the broken shop window. Sgt Smith had watched to see how the young detective coped but when one parent in particular raised his fists then Smith felt obliged to place his bulky frame between the constable and the parents.

"No need for that sir just answer the questions and you can go." Smith was anxious that the young constable could complete his paperwork quickly and get the parents out of the station as quickly as possible. The more cooperative parents, many of whom were very tearful and obviously confused at having to attend a police station, were dealt with by the desk Sgt, These adults held their sons close hoping to save their boys from the bad influence of the rougher kids. But as Sgt Smith said to himself "It's probably too late by now."

Eventually boys and parents were sent home but not before getting a very stern warning from Sgt Smith that if there were any more broken shop windows or any trouble at all in that location the police would know who to look for and their next visit to the station would not be so pleasant. As the door closed Smith heard loud voices as parents continued to yell at their boys. Often that was punctuated by an "Ouch" from a younger voice, evidently some smacked their kids just to reinforce Sgt Smith's warning.

Smith arrived at Jones' office just as the Inspector was putting away his final report of the day.

"Come in Sgt" called Jones. "Did you and P.C. Masters get the youngsters sorted from last evening?"

"Yes we did but oh some of those parents, one or two of the fathers were already known to us and their sons, well sorry to say they looked as though they would be going the same way. The ones I felt sorry for were a couple of the mums who were widows and had younger kids to cope with."

"You'll be putting the report in today?"

"Yes, young Masters has almost finished typing it."

"Good," said Jones "I think that wraps up for today." Just as Sgt Smith began to leave the telephone rang.

"Smith here. Please repeat that. Building site at Baker and Oxford. We're on our way." Turning to Jones, "Kids found a body at the London Road building site Baker and Oxford, by The Level. I'll get the car."

"That'll be the Inspector," said P.C. Stock as another police car drew up beside the crowd. Hurrying across to the new arrivals he pointed to the Ames family as he began to read from his notes. The crowd began to murmur. They knew that the men in the second car were detectives. C.I.D. and word was spreading that the two boys had found a body.

"Must be murder," a woman shouted. Some know-it-all even boasted that they knew who it was.

"Oh yea, bound to 'appen one day. They leave these places open so's anybody can get in," shouted one.

But still the crowd pressed forward to hear more. P.C. Stock finished his report to the detectives and moved back to stand with Mr. Ames and the boys. Jones and Smith crossed the rubble to the body, conferring together. Then suddenly Smith broke away to speak to the uniformed policemen who were holding back the crowd. Suddenly there was movement everywhere; the area was condoned off with rope and stakes leaving just a narrow pathway through the rubble to the body. Another car arrived.

"It must be a murder that's Dr Marshall, the coroner," a loud voice in the crowd claimed. Every piece of rubble was removed from the body and then, after a second look by Jones, the ambulance men were waved forward by Marshall, to remove the body. With the crowd still watching the policemen poked around in the rubble.

"What they looking' for dad?" asked Jimmy.

"Oh just clues. That's what they come for Jimmy."

The Ames family stood waiting knowing the detectives wanted to speak to them. Finally, opening up his notebook, the taller detective came across to the family. Again the curious neighbours tried to move closer to hear the conversation but were brusquely moved back.

"He weren't here yesterday 'cause me and Col. play here every day after school 'til it gets dark. Didn't see nuffink did we Col?" burst out Jimmy, who was on tenterhooks to get his story out. He was breathing very heavily and almost shouting he was so excited at being part of a police drama. What a story he would have to tell his friends at school tomorrow. But he was also nervous about getting into trouble for playing where he had been told not to.

Jones was calm and reassuring as he introduced himself to the parents and then spoke to Jimmy, telling him to slow down.
"You aren't in any trouble lad," he said. "Did you see or hear anyone out here during the night?" he asked both boys. Two heads shook in unison.

"They sleep in the backroom," explained their father. "Besides no decent person would be out here after dark 'because there aren't any lights, although, sometimes tramps build shelters over there beside the wall." Jimmy pointed to the other side of the site where the old bricks from the torn down houses were piled.

"That's where Col and me seen them." But the detective knew that the body was not of a tramp but of a young man, probably not even seventeen years old. Putting away his notebook Jones said,

"Well boys, you did very well today and if you can remember anything else get your dad to bring you down to the station."

Jones thanked the boy's parents for their patience and said that he would be in touch. The boys were sorry to leave but their mother insisted they go home for tea and she hustled them back up the road. Reluctantly the boys followed but each knew that if they could remember just one more thing it would mean a visit to the police station and then a ride home in a police car. So much to tell their mates! It wasn't that they didn't care about the dead young man. They just hadn't recognized him.

Smith ordered two teas as soon as the officers got back to the station. It was a cold, windy autumn evening and he knew it would be at least a couple of hours before they could even think of going home.

"While we wait for tea give me your first impressions," asked Jones as he hung his coat up.

"At first I thought it was just some kid, perhaps even down from London, who had been to the pubs, missed the last train home, taken a kip on the site and just died there."

"My thoughts at first too. What else?"

"Well, although his clothes were muddy and torn at the pockets they were in quite good condition. No darned patches or frayed cuffs."

"Anything that suggested violence to you?" went on Jones, turning to the door as the tea was delivered "Good man. Thanks."

"Nothing definite, he seemed to be just a rather rough looking kid. He certainly had some marks on his face and bruises on his knuckles as if he had been in a fight but nothing that seemed unusual with kids these days".

As Smith drank his tea Jones studied his own notes "We'll go to the morgue in the morning and have a word with Marshall. I want him to have a detailed look at the body. We need to organize a house to house to see if anybody can tell us more about that night and even the day before. See if anybody knows of a lad about that age who has gone missing from around there and be sure to check the Missing Persons reports."

"Right. I'll work on that right away and catch up with you tomorrow after I have sent the lads out." called out Smith as he went to his own office.

Before leaving for the night Jones telephoned Marshall and left a message that he wanted all of the personal effects found on the body to be kept until he arrived the next day and secondly that he wanted a full autopsy done on the body. Earlier Jones had noticed that the bloodstains on the shoulder of the jacket had soaked through to the shirt collar and felt that the beating the lad took could be much more severe than first thought. He was sure that the dead body had more to tell, that the visible bruises were indicative of more than just kids fighting.

Daffyd Jones was thirty-two years old, young to hold the rank of Inspector. He face was long, almost aquiline, carrying a stern look, but when he smiled and displayed his firm white teeth his brown eyes lit up and his face was transformed into one that inspired confidences. Jones wore his dark brown hair longer than the traditional 'short back and sides' style, with one stubborn wave that was always falling down over his forehead, covering the three inch scar that ran over his left eye. A memento of a scrumping adventure with his brothers.

Jones's initial training had been with the York Constabulary where his leadership potential was noted and his rugby prowess was much appreciated. He was twenty-four when he graduated from Hendon Police College and took up a posting with the Liverpool Constabulary as a detective sergeant. One of Jones' team was Stan Butcher, a fellow Military Policeman, who had followed Jones into the Liverpool force. Stan was a product of the meanest streets of East London, and very proud of it. Honest, truthful and wouldn't take any nonsense from anybody. Physically large enough to frighten even the most hardened criminal but always just in his actions. Jones was fascinated by Stan's way of speaking, not just his accent but his flippant disregard for those in authority.

"Bloody hell," he would say to Jones, "What a bunch of idiots sitting up in Whitehall.'Ow do they expect us to catch the criminals if they keep changing their minds on how we should do it? One day it's this and the next day it's that, I wish they would just let us get on with catching and punishing these yobbos."

Jones' favourite expression was Stan's "I could do a better job than that bunch of walleys up there." It was this sense of freedom of expression that Jones' found so fascinating. His parents were so cowed by their life in the Valley that questions were seldom asked and differing opinions never given by those beholden to the mine owners. But here was Stan, a young man with little education, able to give an opinion on all sorts of issues. Jones both envied and admired him for his easy manner and continuous optimism for the future. Stan had been recruited the same time as Jones and an older man Sergeant Adam Fletcher. The three men had gained a reputation of being tough but fair to those who found themselves on the wrong side of the law. They were together on a raid at a small disused factory just north of the city when somebody took a shot at them. Jones and Fletcher managed to duck behind some packing cases but Butcher was not so lucky and he was fatally injured by the ricocheting bullet.

It was a year after Stan's death that Jones moved south to the Sussex Constabulary, while Fletcher took a transfer into the Metropolitan Police to be near his elderly parents.

That evening Jones was a troubled man as he took his customary walk home along the Western Road. He had called Supt Young and mentioned his suspicions about the boy being murdered they would meet up in the morning. But Jones' instinct convinced him the young man had been murdered and wondered what crime had he committed that was so terrible he was killed for it. He wondered if the boy was local, and who were his parents? Was it just an accident or was there something far more sinister waiting to be discovered? Jones was convinced that the young man, whoever he was, had got himself involved, perhaps even accidentally, in something that was too big for him to handle alone and had paid the ultimate price.

CHAPTER TEN

Both officers were in early the next morning. After briefing the Superintendent about the previous evening's events Jones left the station, turned left onto East Street, heading in the direction of the nearby hospital and the morgue. Buckling his raincoat and pulling his trilby down he braced himself for the windy walk across the Old Steine.

Jones loved walking and took full advantage whenever he could. He was still new enough in town that his identity was only known to a few of the many thousands of people who travelled daily through one of the busiest sections of Brighton. The area bounded by West Street and East Street running north to south, and North Street and the seafront going west to east, contained the main southern offices of banks such as Barclays and Lloyds. Solicitors and barristers' offices took up many of the older Regency-style houses while the massive Victorian façade of Hanningtons was the shopping destination of those customers who would never stoop to catch a bus when there were so many taxis available.

Jones was always interested in people and what made them do what they did, especially those in the criminal world. Brighton had a very unique reputation... It was a town almost four hundred years old and had started out as a 'watering hole' for the rich and famous. Over the years as the social offerings changed so did the type of patrons. The arrival of the original steam train service from London and then the electrified service meant that Brighton was only an hour away from London making the town vulnerable to the excesses of London both good and bad... Subsequently many of the London gangs extended not only their criminal activities but also their social positions by taking up a summer residence either in Brighton or in its more upper class neighbour Hove. The racetrack, the large number of antique stores and the secret casinos combined to make the town very attractive to those with money, whether the money was honestly obtained or not, it didn't matter. Brighton couldn't make up its mind what it wanted to be. A town known for entertainment and tourism, which always bought a sleazy side with it, or a quiet, genteel town for refined retirees bringing in lots of money without the hurdy Gordy of tourists.

The summer day trippers were welcomed only if they stayed within a certain area close to the seafront. But Brighton had made itself very attractive to families and with the train journey only an hour away from a dirty and heavily populated capital city, thousands upon thousands of London families made the train journey down every Sunday to enjoy the salt sea breezes and to picnic on the pebbly beach. The internationally famous Brighton Lanes were hidden away in the back streets of this area. Ideally suited to be close at hand for those foreign visitors who stayed in the luxurious hotels that had graced the Esplanade of Brighton for many years, and who revelled in buying so called English Antiques.

Jones kept up a steady pace as he walked on. He was always watchful, noticing little things that he tucked away into his memory for future reference. Such things, as the men cleaning Hannington's great windows, he would take note of the name on their van. As he would note any lorries that seemed to be parked for an excessive time, especially those near a Bank. As he crossed the grassy lawns of the Old Steine he would check out any loiterers and move on any drunks who had decided to sleep out of doors. But mainly he would use this time to breathe in the salty air and think of the cases on his desk, being especially grateful that his Super had encouraged his participation in the Network project.

"The more we can do to keep those elements away from our patch the better," was Young's comment. When Jones spoke informally about the needed resources and the time that he himself would need to carry any plan forward, the Super appeared to be in agreement.

"Just get the plan going, check it with the Yard and we'll see," he had said.

When Jones reached the bottom of St. James's Street he turned into Joe Lyon's Corner Restaurant. This was one of his favourite places for a morning cup of coffee. From a certain table, just inside the entrance, he had an excellent view across the Old Steine and Castle Square. He could watch as the green Southdown buses negotiated the narrow entrance into Pool Valley, and beyond the Royal Albion Hotel he could just glimpse the blue, green water of the Channel.

Whenever Jones managed to drop in for a coffee there was always the same man sitting at a nearby table who smiled and doffed his cap to him. Jones always nodded but not one word was exchanged between the two men. Jones vowed that one day he would find out who this man was.

Sipping his coffee his thoughts returned to sadness he felt at the sight of the young man's body lying in all that dirt and rubble... He was surprised by his own reaction, assuming he'd grown immune to violent sights, had become hardened to body parts lying around. In a way he was pleased that he could still feel compassion. Although Brighton was a city more to be compared to the noise and brashness of Blackpool than to the quiet, genteel elegance of perhaps Hove or Eastbourne, finding a body just lying around was a very rare occurrence.

By the time Jones arrived at the mortuary Sgt Smith had caught up with him and together they pushed the swing doors open and stepped into the tiled and antiseptic domain of the pathologist. Dr Marshall was waiting for them and with a curt "Morning," he began to recite what he had found so far relating to the young corpse.

"Age, approximately 17 years, build-slight not used to manual work, no callouses on hands, well-nourished and could have been athletic."

"Right," said Jones, "cause of death?"

"An interesting case!" went on Marshall "no exterior wounds bad enough to cause death and other than everyday scrapes nothing on the face or hands." Before Jones could voice another question Marshall pulled back the sheet fully "But look here," he said and pointed out to the officers numerous bruises and cigarette burn marks on the torso.

"And", continued Marshall, "We have discovered five broken ribs, two broken fingers as well as tears in his spleen, liver and kidneys."

For a moment there was silence in the room as both policemen realized that this was no ordinary death and the victim must have suffered incredible pain before dying.

"And cause of death then Dr?" asked Jones, looking away from the broken body.

"My report will show that this young man suffered a brutal beating that damaged his internal organs, causing massive internal bleeding and ultimately death."

"Anything on his clothing?"

"Nothing special," said the Dr, "ordinary trousers and jacket. Not expensive, usual clothing kids wear these days. But he did have quite a fancy shirt on as though he was having a night out."

"Thank you Rd. How soon can you have the report on my desk?" asked Jones.

"I will send it over this afternoon." Marshall replied.

The two men left the mortuary deep in thought. While Sgt Smith was concentrating on the logistics of a murder inquiry and how to get the operation under way, the Inspector's thoughts were about why the boy had been killed and where this investigation would lead them. This would be the first time that he and Smith would work together on a murder case. They had worked on accidental deaths such as drownings and road accidents and many assault and battery cases, but a murder inquiry was so different. The walk back to the office was quiet as each man considered his part in moving this murder investigation forward.

Smith had not been overly pleased when Jones was brought into the Sussex Constabulary. Both the Chief Inspector of Detectives and his Superintendent had retired at the same time and the promotions necessary to fill those positions had left a vacancy at the Inspector rank. Smith did not expect a promotion but having spent so many years in the force and being more or less in charge of procedures he had been very apprehensive about the future. He had heard about Jones' earlier training and his successful investigations in Liverpool and it bothered him that Jones might come in like some kind of whizz kid demanding immediate changes in a system of routines and procedures that had served Smith and the station, for many years.

It took Smith a few weeks to feel at ease with the younger man. Jones was different than he had expected, not displaying any officiousness that Smith expected from a former military officer and although not a man ready to exchange personal confidences Jones was friendly and respectful to the older, more experienced Smith. Smith was surprised that Jones took time to sit with him and listen while Smith showed his new boss the requisite forms and the system of communication used throughout headquarters and how the many substations dotted around the County were connected.

Eventually together, they did create a new system for reporting incidents and an easier system for filing reports. This was what Smith excelled at and feeling more at ease with Jones, Smith happily took on the responsibility of training all personal in the new procedures. This new partnership between the sometimes ponderous, master of detail and process, older man and the instinctive, people oriented younger man resulted in a good working relationship that produced positive results.

In fact, Smith reflected as they crossed East Street, *The only fly in the ointment is that young know-it–all Masters.* But Smith kept this observation to himself as he knew that given time and his paternal guidance even young Masters would eventually be a credit to the Force.

CHAPTER ELEVEN

Mrs. Williams hurried along the hallway; she really didn't need these interruptions just now. The table was set. The little girls were seated waiting for their father to come down, and the food was already on the table.

It was young Bert standing there in the doorway.

"Hello Mrs. Williams I was wondering if Bobby was alright?"

"Come in Bert," Mrs. Williams closed the door behind him. "We haven't seen our Bobby since he left for the pub on Monday evening. We thought he had work and was away for a couple of days."

"I dunno Mrs. Williams. I did see him getting into a black van outside the pub and now its Wednesday and he still hasn't been around. It's not like Bobby; he always tells me when he's going off. I asked around but nobody has seen him." Clearly Bert was worried about his friend. Mrs. Williams tried to reassure him,

"Oh Bert we both know that our Bobby is always looking out for quick money. I expect a job came up and he'll be home in a couple of days. "But her words bought little comfort to Bert who just stood in the kitchen, hands in pockets wondering where his friend was.

"Now you get home for dinner Bert and when Mr. Williams comes down I'll tell him why you were here and he'll know what to do." As she was ushering a rather reluctant Bert out of the house she heard her husband's step on the stairs and his voice calling,

"Who was at the door then?"

"It was young Bert, you know Bobby's friend. He hasn't seen Bobby since Monday and he wondered if he was ill or something."

"Well he's not here for sure, is he?" he asked as he sat at the table, "when did you last see him then, you see more of him than I do. What do you think?"

"Perhaps I should go to the police station just in case he's been in an accident or something."

"Yes," agreed Mr. Williams "but let's leave it for a couple of days I expect he'll turn up."

"As you say dear."

"There," she said to the girls, "I expect he'll be home tomorrow."

Jones was waiting for Sgt Smith to bring him up to date on the results of the house-to-house investigation. It was a highly populated area and had taken two officers over two days to get to every citizen. None of the householders questioned had seen anything untoward Monday evening; one man walking his dog had seen a black van leaving the end of the street going towards St. Peter's Church at about ten thirty. The men walking home from the pub just around the corner from the building site had been able to confirm each other's activities, especially as most of them had played darts together. So apart from a possible black van the inquiries produced very little.

The Inspector was very troubled that no one had reported the boy missing. There had been no news from other stations regarding any missing youth... Perhaps, as Smith had suggested, he was here on holiday, perhaps a runaway, perhaps he was even a foreigner and they would never have a name for him. Dr. Marshall's autopsy report had confirmed the essence of their conversation that death was as a result of a severe beating. Jones had reported as much to his Superintendent who agreed to keep the investigation on but if no progress had been made after two weeks then the boy had to be buried and the case put into the Unsolved File.

It was about two o'clock that afternoon when the first break in the case came. A middle-aged woman had come into the police station to report that her son, Bobby, had not been home for several days. The desk sergeant took down the details and was about to send the woman home with a re-assuring, "I'll expect he'll be home soon," when he remembered the notice he had sent out to the other stations. He quickly asked the woman to take a seat and hurriedly called Jones and explained... Within minutes Jones and Smith were accompanying the anxious woman to an interview room. Smith ordered a cup of tea and the presence of a policewoman. As the woman was hustled down into the inner workings of the station she became more and more distressed and insisted that they call her husband who was at home asleep, after his night shift. Sgt Smith arranged for P.C. Masters to take a car and pick up Mr. Williams for both he and Jones suspected that these innocent parents were going to face a difficult time ahead. Once they had Mrs. Williams settled Jones began by asking her about her son, to tell him what kind of boy he was.

"He's just turned seventeen been out of school about a year. Well he weren't one for school, too many rules and he didn't like the bookwork. We had the attendance officer around several times because our Bobby had skipped school. Bobby is always a happy lad, he has many friends and he's always laughing and joking around. My Bobby loves football and went to see Arsenal as often as he could. He was up there just last weekend. He took his mates up in a car and every Saturday he was really keen to do the results for his dad's Pools."

"Did he have regular work?" asked Jones. He had moved his chair closer to Mrs. Williams, trying to make the conversation as friendly as possible while Smith sat in the background taking notes. "I wondered how he got the money to travel up to London regularly".

"That's exactly what his father wanted to know," she answered. "His father was always asking where his money came from for football and for some of his fancy shirts, but Bobby's answer was always the same, "Oh dad I helped this bloke out on a couple of jobs." he'd say."

"What kind of jobs Mrs. Williams?"

"He told 'is dad they were all building jobs but I know different. Sometimes he works for a bookie at the racetrack and sometimes he did window cleaning. One time, when he was away for three days, he said that he had been painting big houses up country. But I knew he had been lying to me as paint smells and there weren't no smell about Bobby. But my Bobby never did any 'arm to anyone, 'e loves his game of darts and sometimes looks after the girls when his dad and I go out to play whist at the church."

Just then P.C. Masters arrived with a very sleepy looking Mr. Williams who greeted his wife with "What's all this about then, what's the boy been up to?" turning to Jones he said, "That young constable won't tell me anything at all; just that I was needed down at the station."

"Thank you for coming in Mr. Williams, I just need to confirm a few more details with you about your son Bobby. Do drink your cup of tea. Did Bobby go to the pub at all?"

"Oh yes he loves his games of darts, he's pretty good at it too. That's the last time I saw him when he left for his darts game last Monday night at the Black Swan. I really didn't take much notice of him being away as he does jobs up country and with me working the night shift it could be a few days before Bobby and me had a chance to chat." William's shoulders began to sag, "But when young Bert came around to see us and said as how Bobby had missed the darts match that Monday and Bert hadn't seen him since. Well I began to think about where he could be. 'Course he talks to his mum a lot but she didn't know either." said Williams, looking across at his wife.

Jones handed Williams a pad of paper, "Please write the names and addresses of Bobby's closest friends, those that go to the pub and to soccer with him."

"You better do it luv, you know the kids better that I do." Mrs. Williams's hands were shaking as she took the pencil from her husband.

"I don't know the proper numbers for all of them," she explained hesitantly.

"That's alright," said Smith. "We'll figure it out."

By now Mrs. Williams had sensed that something was very wrong. She was visibly restless and agitated and had to lean heavily on the desk to complete her list. Suddenly she lifted her head pleading.

"Why don't you just tell us what's wrong? Why are we here and where is our Bobby?" In an effort to calm her Jones asked about their other children and softly, Mrs. Williams answered, "Yes we have three little girls, they're at school, but Bobby is our only boy, our eldest."

There was a discreet knock on the door, Masters entered, whispered to Smith and left closing the door softly behind him. Jones saw the interaction between the two and began.

"Mr. and Mrs. Williams I am sorry to have to tell you that we may have some very distressing news for you. Last Tuesday evening, the body of a young man was found on the building site at the back of the Co-op on London Road. The young man did not have any identification on him but the general physical description does fit that of your boy Bobby. I am very sorry but I have to ask you to come along to the mortuary with us to tell us if the body is that of your son."

Mrs. Williams collapsed in her chair, sobbing uncontrollably still hanging on to the arm of the policewoman. Mr. Williams was sitting upright, looking ahead as if he had been turned to stone. For a few minutes the only sound was of sobbing, even the general busyness of the outside corridor had ceased. Smith quietly opened the door and stood patiently waiting. Gently Jones helped Williams to his feet and taking him by the arm escorted him into the corridor. Mrs. Williams, holding tightly to her handbag and being supported by the policewoman, followed slowly behind as the small procession made its way down the corridor to the waiting cars.

The parents were helped into the back seat of the first car and Jones sat with the driver. Smith and the WPC climbed into the other car. It was only a short drive over to the mortuary but neither officer spoke during the journey, each occupied with their own thoughts. Dr Marshall had been informed about their impending arrival and was waiting just inside the entrance as the cars arrived. Jones introduced him and Mr. Williams nodded but both parents were so visibly afraid of what they had to face, they clung together for strength and little else mattered.

The antiseptic smell that pervades all hospitals became much heavier as the group moved further into the basement to a small waiting room. Marshall explained that they could wait here until they felt ready to go in and view the body.

"Whenever you feel up to it," added Marshall going through to the next room. Mr. Williams immediately stood up, straightened his shoulders and said.

"Let's get this over with." Turning to his wife "You best stay here luv with the Sgt" Smith had volunteered to stay behind with her but Mrs. Williams insisted on seeing her son.

"No. I have to see if it's our Bobby. I have to be there to see. I'll never rest if I don't see him this last time."

Taking her husband's arm they stepped forward together through the second door into the mortuary. The officers flanked the parents as they moved slowly across the room to where a green-coated mortuary assistant waited beside a stretcher. Looking at Jones for permission he slowly pulled down the sheet to expose the marble face of the young man.

A sharp intake of breath and a broken sob gave Jones his answer. At first Mr. Williams was transfixed at the sight of his only son lying there, and then he began shouting and swearing until his wife took his arm and whispered.

"Hush now dear Bobby wouldn't like to hear you like that." Then she moved closer to her dead son and gently ran her fingers down the boy's cheek. At first her hand trembled and she lifted it quickly but then she touched the cold flesh again and stood for a moment grasping Bobby's hand in hers.

"Yes," she said to Jones, "this is our Bobby. Isn't it dear?" Her husband looked at her and then moved to her side and placed his hand on Bobby's hair, ruffling it.

"Yes it is our Bobby."

Fresh tea had been brought in to the waiting room and for several minutes nothing was said. Then, with apologies Jones asked Mr. Williams to confirm that the body they had seen was that of their son Bobby. Both parents nodded in agreement.

Dr.. Marshall then asked Mr. Williams to sign the official identity form and left the room. Gently Jones spoke,

"On behalf of Brighton Police I offer our sincere condolences on the loss of your son, also, for having to ask you to come here to identify him." Pausing, he then asked if they had any questions. Mrs. Williams wanted to know more details about how Bobby had died and Jones explained as gently as possible that Bobby did have bruises on his body and his death was listed as being suspicious.

"Did he suffer?" she whispered.

"No" lied Jones explaining "the pathologist explained that he would have slipped into a coma and then passed away."

"Why would anyone want to kill my Bobby?" she asked, more to herself than to the others. Jones sat ready to answer any questions but he couldn't answer that one. Not yet anyway.

"Anything else?" said the father and not waiting for a reply stood up, picked up his cap, took his wife by the arm and said in a soft voice, "Missus and me are going home now. We got the little ones to look after."

Jones explained that the police would contact whichever funeral parlour they wanted and their son's body would be moved there as soon as arrangements were made. Jones also said that he would call on them tomorrow.

A car was provided for their trip home and accompanied by W.P.C. Hart, the stunned parents left.

CHAPTER TWELVE

It was Saturday morning; family shopping day for the majority of people and Jones was revisiting the building site. It was something he needed to do before going to keep his appointment with Mr. and Mrs. Williams. Now he knew who the boy was he could look at the place of death with a different focus. He needed to confirm that his men had not missed anything but more than that he wanted to get some first-hand experience of the neighbourhood knowing that even the passing traffic could give him a clue why Bobby's body was dumped at this particular spot. He had asked Smith to pick him up at two o'clock when they would go and see if the parents would allow him to see Bobby's room.

Jones began by taking a walking tour of the neighbouring streets. He really had very little expectations of finding anything new but he felt he owed Bobby something, after all his murder had taken place on his 'patch' and though no fault of Jones Bobby had lain in the mortuary for several days without anyone to mourn over him. *"It's not right, that's not the way life is supposed to work out for a young man,"* thought Jones. Spending time at the last known resting place of the young man was the least he could do.

The small terraced houses opened directly on to the pavement. No gardens at the front although some creative tenants had placed tubs of flowers to pretty up their entrance way. The houses, in the main, were painted different colours in an effort to gain some individuality but others were simply there, no flowers, no new paint and no bright curtains. Walking down Oxford Street Jones noticed that for some reason this side of the building site was totally fenced in with large signs warning residents not to trespass unlike the other side which was open to anyone. Jones made a note to call the Town Corporation and find out why this site had been left open.

The back gardens of the houses were long and narrow with a concrete path leading to a shed at the end and accessible by a common back alley between the back entrances. Many of the householders were still cultivating their own vegetable gardens; some still had their bean sticks up from summer. One or two even had chicken coups and runs with a cockerel strutting around making a noise. Every house had a washing line and used other space to store bikes, wheelbarrows and such. Both Baker and Oxford ran from The Level to the London Road, which was the main shopping area for the working class citizens of Brighton. The big name shops such as The Co-op, Bellmans and Woolworths with their large windows, were surrounded by numerous smaller businesses. Jewellers, cobblers, ironmongers, wool shops and many others, all jostled side by side to attract customers. There were people everywhere, rushing in or out of shops, queuing up at the corner greengrocers, and some running, with loaded shopping bags, for the many red buses that were so frequent along London Road. He watched the constable on duty at the zebra crossing and then, as he continued his tour he came upon the narrow entrance to the Open Market.

Walking past Dawkin's blacksmith's shop with its ancient horse stock, he was soon enveloped in the sounds, smells and noise of the Market traders. The smell of freshly caught local fish, the warm enticing aroma of frying bacon reminded Jones that he hadn't eaten since breakfast. He watched at the brightly coloured fruit and vegetable stalls where traders whipped bags of apples or pears so swiftly off the scales many shoppers never saw the true weight. The traders, both men and women, were artists in their own right, they knew how to attract shoppers, how to sell goods that were dented.

"Oh fell off the lorry luv, look nuffing wrong with it. How about two for the price of one then?" or

"I dug these potatoes out myself, wif me own hands. Look take the potatoes and I'll frow in these greens for nothing. Can't beat that can yer?"

Jones noticed that not all of the shoppers, who were mostly housewives, were taken in with the trader's patter and were master barterers themselves going from stall to stall until they were satisfied with the deal they had made.

It was a cold morning with many stallholders wearing heavy coats under the traditional apron. Some held steaming cups of tea in their mittened hands as they continually watched the crowd for prospective customers. When a likely customer came close they quickly put down their mugs of tea, walked to the front and started their patter. Often the human voices were in competition with the animals that owners hoped to sell. The unwanted kittens and puppies, the soft and cuddly rabbits, the odd goat or two waited in their cages for a new owner, their damp straw adding yet another odour to the mix. As Jones moved through the throng of shoppers to the north end there were a gathering of stalls, or just tables, offering such diverse items as bicycles or even just bits of cycles, odd shaped pieces of leather, used furniture, straw, even bags of manure.

"Always good for the garden mate," sang out one man as the Inspector passed by.

Jones stopped at a stall for tea. He had seen a couple of older men sitting chatting at a table and asked if he could join them. After introducing himself and getting the usual.

"Not from around here then are you?" to his Welsh accent, he asked about the local kids, the teenagers in particular. He wanted to know if there were any gangs or any other problems usually associated with kids around this area. The two men had heard about the body and were anxious to know more but accepted that the investigation was moving along rather slowly. Both men said how sad it was that the boy did not have an opportunity to grow up,

"It just isn't right," muttered one man as the other said

"Just make sure you catch those who did it."

Otherwise they said that the local kids were often noisy and stole from the stalls but really nothing that the local constable couldn't handle. Thanking them Jones went back out to the bordering streets. He wanted to take a closer look at the back alleys to see if there were any signs of blood or weapons that could have been used on Bobby. Although Marshall had stated that Bobby was not killed at the site they had no clue as to where he was murdered.

Overall, his visit and his conversation over tea just confirmed to Jones what he already thought. The neighbourhood was made up of people who were working hard just to survive. Many were families of three or four, often with relatives living close by, there were also at least ten older widows whose children had left home for better opportunities. Many of the men worked for the Brighton Corporation or on the Southern Railway in the marshalling yards up on New England Road. Some of the mums also worked, the majority were either 'clippies' working on the corporation buses or they were fortunate enough to get in at the big Allan West factory just along Lewes Road. Jones was sure that when he and Smith went up to the Williams' house the neighbourhood would be identical.

As he walked back towards The Level looking for Smith with the car an older man stopped him.

"You're the Inspector aren't you?" and when Jones nodded the man continued, "I don't know if you remember me but I spoke to you and the Sgt about spotting a black van the night before that young man's body was found."

He said that his name was Ernest Plant and explained that he'd planned to visit Jones at the police station the next morning but now this chance meeting would save him a journey.

"I remembered something about that evening. It was something in the back of my mind all along but I just couldn't bring it out. But, suddenly as I was walking past the place this morning I remembered." Jones asked him to go through step by step what he remembered.

"I was walking along and Peggy, my dog, was sniffing along the edge of the pavement. It was late and very dark, as the street lights were not working properly, when suddenly these bright headlights went on just ahead of me, only about a yard ahead. I told the sergeant that but what I didn't remember was that just moments before I had felt a sort of puffing beside me and I realized that the van must have started off in the gutter but not put the lights on until it was well out into the road. The driver wouldn't have seen me because by then I was behind him and they raced off very quickly."

Jones thanked him and asked if he would mind going to the station and making a statement. The older man was pleased to do that.

"Crying shame leaving a lad to die like that-you make sure you get them," he said as he resumed his walk.

Just then the police car drew up beside Jones and he hopped in.

"Well" he asked "How did you get on with the boys?"

While he had been out walking Sgt Smith and P.C. Masters were involved in questioning the three boys who were Bobby's closest friends. It was Smith's intention that the boys would be interviewed individually at first and then together. Smith knew that teenage boys were the most difficult to question. Not because they were deliberately obstructive but more because they didn't realize the importance of even the tiniest bit of information or occurrence. It had been Smith's experience that letting the boys chat together had often produced vital clues. P.C. Masters offered some resistance to this plan suggesting, in a respectful tone.

"Surely it would be better to frighten the life out of the boys so that they would speak up".

Smith was well aware of the young policeman's stern and sometimes officious attitude towards the younger population and he wanted to use this exercise to show Masters a better way to of communicate with young people. Smith had grunted to himself when he heard Masters' opinion. The constable himself was only twenty-five.

Smith had everything organized when the boys and parents arrived. He was determined that Masters, with his prompting, would be the lead using a 'friendlier' style of questionings.

"Of the three boys we talked to," Smith told Jones, "Bert had the most to tell us. Bert considered himself Bobby's best friend as they spent time together each day. He told us that he was supposed to meet Bobby at the Black Swan at 8.o'clock that Monday night. They had an important darts tournament and they reminded each other of the match just as they got off the bus".

"So what happened?"

"Bert said that he arrived a little early and saw Bobby getting into a black van just along the road from the pub. I asked him if Bobby looked to be in trouble and Bert said he didn't think so, in fact Bobby gave him a double thumbs-up sign through the window and then the van drove off."

"Has Bert seen Bobby since?

"No but Bert said that Bobby did sometimes go off for a few days on some kind of job or other but he was always back for the Monday night darts game."

"Could he describe the van?"

"Small, black and there were two men."

"Any description of the men?"

"Only that one looked to be very large. But then Bert said something that I found interesting. He thought that he'd seen the large man before. Bert was sure that the man was seated at the back of the bus that he and Bobby caught to go home for tea."

"Did he have any idea where this man had got on the bus?" asked Jones

"I did ask him and he said he thought somewhere around the Steine, Bert said he didn't see him when the boys went upstairs but saw him a little later when Bert said he turned round to see what was on at the Astoria."

"I wonder if we have a connection," sighed Jones. "A large man seen on Bobby's bus and then again with the van picking up Bobby, perhaps the same van that was seen late Monday night. What do you think Sgt?"

"It would take two men, at least, to hold a strong lad like Bobby down. How about you sir, did you find anything new?" Smith asked.

"Not really. The area is as we thought, full mostly of ordinary folk, hardworking just trying to improve things for their families. No real trouble with the youngsters, mostly it's just bits of mischief the kids get up to. Oh, I did have another conversation with the man who saw a black van near in the area Monday evening, a Mr. Plant. He'll come in tomorrow to make a statement," finished Jones.

While Smith drove, Jones described the things they should focus on with Bobby's parents Smith agreed but suggested that while Jones went upstairs to look at the boy's bedroom he would stay downstairs with Mrs. Williams.

"Mums often know far more about their boys than they let on to their husbands," Smith explained, knowingly.

Dealing with a murder inquiry was a new experience for both officers and when the victim was so young and obviously so well loved both men knew that they had to tread very carefully throughout the investigation. As Smith knocked it was quickly opened by Mr. Williams.

"The missus saw the car and put the kettle on. Please come into the front room," he said ushering the two men through the doorway.

But Smith went towards the kitchen, "I'll just give Mrs. Williams a hand," he called as he walked down the hallway... Jones sat down in one of the spacious armchairs and looked around at the good solid furniture that filled the room.

“How are you Mr. Williams?” he asked.

“Not bad. Difficult to understand why anybody would do this to our Bobby. Very difficult for the girls, I don’t think they have any idea of what’s happened. They think Bobby ‘ll be home soon.” Mr. Williams turned his head away and just stared out of the window. Smith came in with a tea tray, placing it on the small table. Mrs. Williams followed; she looked very pale and tired and staggered a little as she sat down heavily in her chair.

“I’ll help you all I can but I spend most of my day crying. I can’t get over that our Bobby was lying in that cold room all by himself with nobody knowing he was there. It’s not right,” she cried.

Smith took charge of pouring tea and asking what seemed to be very mundane questions as he handed out each cup. Jones was very impressed by Smith’s warmth and kindness as he took care of Mrs. Williams, making sure her tea was fine, that she was comfortable and complimenting her on the home made cake. Jones himself was almost overwhelmed by the deep sadness and grief that had enveloped these two very ordinary people. He found his mouthful of tea very difficult to swallow quickly putting his cup down unsure he even hold that securely...

Like the bereaved father he sat and stared out of the window while Smith settled himself in the armchair beside Bobby’s mother. Mrs. William’s sister had stayed with the couple most of yesterday and returned early this morning to take the little girls to the park while the officers were in the house. Gathering himself Jones asked permission to have a look at Bobby’s bedroom. He and Mr. Williams went upstairs while, as planned, Smith stayed down with Mrs. Williams offering to pour her another tea and gently coaxing more answers from the broken woman.

Although very tidy with the bed made and clothes put away, it was still a typical young man’s bedroom. Posters of football’s great adorned the walls, there was a pile of American style comics on the dresser along with a record player.

“What did Bobby listen to?” Jones asked.

“Oh, like the kids today it was all about noise. He liked the older big band sound and he even went to see the last concert by Joe Loss when he came to Brighton last summer. Bobby used to go to the dance halls he was a great one for dancing."

"I see that he supported Arsenal. Why a London team Mr. Williams?"

"Well we still have family around London and Bobby didn't have much time for the third division teams here in town. Thought the 'Seagulls' should have been much better than they were. He wouldn't even come with me on a Saturday afternoon. Now he'll never come."

Mr. Williams sat down heavily on his son's bed dropping his head into his hands and began silently to rock to and fro. Jones continued to look around the room. Bending down he picked up some odd items that were lying beside the bed. It was the program from the Arsenal v Chelsea game with the entrance ticket stub caught inside the front page. Jones opened drawers and searched the wardrobe but found nothing out of the ordinary. He glanced up to look at the model airplanes on the shelf, as a boy he too had enjoyed making models. Then suddenly something caught his eye. He stood against the wardrobe and running his hands along the top felt the outline of a box. Lifting it down he saw it was, similar to those made by boys in school carpentry classes, he asked Mr. Williams if he would like to open it. Slowly Mr. Williams opened his son's treasure box. Inside held by a rubber band lay a fat bundle of ten pound notes.

"Oh my God where did he get those?" whispered Mr. Williams. He flew down the stairs calling to his wife.

"Betty look what Bobby had upstairs. Did you know he had all this money?" By her face Jones knew that she was as shocked as her husband.

"No, I never saw that money before," and started to weep softly into her handkerchief.

Leaving a receipt for the money and taking a recent photograph of Bobby, the officers thanked the couple, offering any help when needed and quietly let themselves out the house just as the girls were returning home. Both officers greeted the girls and held the garden gate open as they skipped in the door obviously pleased to be home.

The two men sat in the car and it was a while before Jones spoke, asking Smith if he had learnt anything more from Mrs. Williams.

"Yes a couple of things. Apparently about a week ago, before the boys went to London, Bobby had been looking for something that he felt should have been in the local paper. He never told his mum what he was looking for but Mrs. Williams said that he seemed very upset that it wasn't in the paper."

"It must have been something that he knew about and perhaps he was involved in," asked Jones.

"Perhaps" said Smith "but she mentioned that a few days before that Bobby's dad had asked him what work he had done when he stayed out all night. Bobby had said that he helped at a fire in the Savoy but she said she never smelt any smoke on any of Bobby's clothes."

"It sounds to me that there was more to young Bobby Williams than we know about. Anything else?"

"Yes, that Bobby had his eye on a girl who lived a couple of streets over. They were part of a larger group of kids who had been friends at school and still hung out together. According to Mum Bobby had never taken her out on a real date but she could tell that he was sweet on her," said Smith.

"You have a name?"

"Yes, Pamela Watts, she lives at number thirty-five just down here," Smith pointed to a house with a dark blue front door.

"Let's go and see if she is in," said Jones.

Both Pamela and her mother were in and after showing Mrs. Watts their warrant cards and explaining why they had called Mrs. Watts invited the officers in.

"Pamela is still very upset about Bobby but I will try and get her to come downstairs and talk to you," she said.

"Thank you," said Jones, "we'll try not to upset her any further".

Mrs. Watts went halfway up the stairs and called her daughter to come down. Soon they heard a door slowly open and a slight, dark haired, pretty girl came down the stairs into the sitting room. The officers stood as she came in and introduced themselves. She was about seventeen years old, nicely dressed but her eyes were red-rimmed with crying.

"Thank you for seeing us'" said Jones. "We would like to ask you some questions about Bobby Williams. Do you feel up to helping us?"

She nodded. Smith started, "Pamela. We are so sorry about young Bobby's death but your name was given to us as being a particular friend of Bobby's is that so and how well did you know him?"

"We went to school together since Form three and then when we finished school six of us who live around here still chummed together," explained the young woman.

"Your Mum was telling us that you have a job in the bakery." Pam nodded,

"Yes I work the early morning shift."

Smith continued, "Do you know what Bobby did during the daytime?"

"I only saw him a couple of evenings a week and then at the weekends. If I asked what he had been doing he always joked around and said that he had been doing special jobs for rich people."

"Pamela, we now know that Bobby's death was deliberate, do you know of any reason or have any information that led you to think that he was in any danger?" asked Jones.

She shook her head, "I was always telling him to get a regular job," she sobbed, "and stop having these wild schemes to get rich quick. I don't know where he got his money. I know his parents didn't have much to give him." Pamela suddenly stopped talking, took a deep breath while looking at her mother. "Bobby loved to drive, he didn't have a license but, Bobby had an old car, a brown Hillman. I haven't seen it since Bobby went missing."

"Where did he keep it?" asked Smith

"Down at the back of Bill's house. He didn't use it much but he took care of it and we went out for a ride a couple of times. I went down to see if it was still there as Bobby hadn't been round this week. But it's gone." Pamela explained.

"Can you remember any details about the car? It might help if we could find it."

"I don't know the number on the bottom but it was mainly brown. One of the doors was rusty so Bobby covered it with some kind of grey special paint. It had four doors and always reminded me of getting into a taxi." Jones and Smith exchanged glances. Jones continued.

"Pamela we found a large amount of money in Bobby's bedroom do you have any idea how he would have got that?" Pam hesitated, twisting her handkerchief as again she looked at her mother. She had more to tell but was torn between loyalty to her dead friend and helping the police. She moved to sit closer to her mother who murmured to her that it would be much better if she told all that she knew. "Bobby did not deserve to die like that and the police need to catch the killers." Pam lifted her shoulders. "There's a gang of kids on the Whitehawk estate who were always giving us trouble."

"What kind of trouble and why?" asked Smith.

"Well they're mostly about the same age as us and sometimes last year we used to meet at the swings on the Racehill and they were always pushing and shoving us off the swings and roundabouts. Once they pushed me and I fell and split my knee open. A couple of years ago some London kids moved here and one of those boys sort of became their leader. One day Bobby and he had a big fight so these days we try to avoid them but they often come over here to the local clubs making trouble."

"Any particular reason?" asked Jones, looking hard at the young girl. Pamela face went pink and she looked at her mother. The girl was embarrassed and looked down at her hands as she explained to the policemen that the leader of the Whitehawk gang wanted her to be his girlfriend and t if she didn't go with him he was going to get Bobby. She looked up. "Sometimes when we met they would shout horrible things at me. Maggie would call me a tart or a slut and they would call Bobby a thief and other bad things. We stopped going to some places in case we met them.

"Was Bobby afraid of them?"

"No. He called them London trash and told me not to take any notice. But it wasn't very nice so that's why we went to different places," Pam said.

"When did you last meet up?"

"A couple of Saturdays ago when we were all at the roller rink on the seafront. As soon as Bert saw Tom and Maggie we all left."

"So Tom is the leader and Maggie?"

"She's his younger sister."

“Pamela we are very sorry about Bobby and what you have told us has been very helpful. Would you write down the names and addresses, if you know them, of the Whitehawk group?” Smith handed Pamela a pad of paper.

“Do you think they killed Bobby?” asked Mrs. Watts.

“We are certainly going to visit them to see what they have to say for themselves.” answered Jones as he collected the list from Pamela and prepared to leave. Suddenly he stopped and turned to the young girl, “Did Bobby ever tell you about any jobs that he had been on recently?”

For a moment she looked very scared, then hesitantly told the men that Bobby had told her about being asked to do a special job over in Rottingdean. “He was so pleased he’d been asked. He was only the driver but he said the pay was good. Bobby said there were three of them.”

“Any idea when this was or what house?”

“Yes it was about two weeks ago and the house was a large one, not too far from the windmill.”

By now Pamela was distraught and her mother was not having much success at calming her down. The officers thanked Mrs. Watts for letting them in and asked her to bring Pamela down to the police station to sign a statement of everything she had told them and to add any more things she remembered.

“Thank you again.” said Jones.

Smith told Mrs Watts that he would arrange a car for Monday. “They will pick you up about ten o’clock.” Mrs. Watts nodded in agreement and closed the door.

Back at the office Jones suggested that as it was almost half past five that Smith go home to his family.

“I’ll stay and tidy up my notes and then Monday first thing, we will sit down and plan our next step.” Jones was in no hurry to pack up for the night, in fact he was feeling very excited at the gains they had made this day and finally he could see a connection between events. He began a list of what they knew; two black vans seen at two locations. Or was it the same van seen twice? The large man seen on the bus, the bundle of tenners in Bobby’s possession, two more thieves in on the robbery and Bobby’s mysterious missing car, and what was Bobby looking for in the paper? Could it be connected in any way with the other robberies?

CHAPTER THIRTEEN

The weekend had been hectic at the station, gang fights on the beach, a robbery at Sherry's dance hall and a wedding celebration that got out of hand as some extremely drunken guests decided that midnight at high tide was a good time to go swimming. Consequently, the overnight cells were full and the paperwork, interviews and visiting solicitors took up most of Sunday.

First thing Monday morning Smith thoroughly checked the in-coming reports for anything about a recent robbery in Rottingdean, but no such report existed. Next Smith went to Jones' office to lay out his plan for the day..

"P.C. Masters has listed all the serial numbers on Bobby's banknotes and has taken them across to Barclays and Lloyds to see if they can help us out with the numbers. Two constables are checking lists of automobile registrations to see how many black vans are registered in the county. A car and driver are on their way to pick up Mrs. Watts and Pamela to sign their statements and I'm sending an officer from another team over to there to chat with the sergeant. Oh yes I have sent out a memo to all substations to be on the lookout for Bobby's missing car. That's all so far," explained Smith. "

"That's a good start. "said Jones:" Oh Bobby's funeral will be Friday at eleven." added Smith.

"Thanks, we will go and pay our respects. In the meantime I want to visit every member of the so-called Whitehawk gang starting with the brother and sister. You have all the names and addresses. We could start later this afternoon when the kids should be in for their tea?" Smith left. He had lots to do and he felt hopeful somewhere amongst all these leads they would find Bobby's killer.

Lying on the Inspector's desk was the usual pile of memos and as he flipped through the yellow sheets he spotted one marked 'Urgent-very Urgent' that had been buried in the. An elderly lady had reported that a black van had been parked outside her house for more than a week and she wanted to know when it was going to be moved. This was her second complaint and she wanted a policeman out there at once to move it, as it was blocking her view. If it wasn't moved soon she would call her Member of Parliament.

Jones called in Smith "Where is this Clermont Terrace?"

"It's along my way, right outside Preston Park Station. Why?" Jones showed him the memo.

"We should get out there right away and check this out. It's the only abandoned black van to be reported," he said.

"Right," said Smith," according to the memo the old lady doesn't have a telephone, but she's bound to be in at this time of day. It's a very quiet, residential area, part of the Old Preston Village. Full of solicitors and doctors and people who work in London

Jones called down to the garage "I need a black van picked up at Clermont Terrace. Now. Bring it to the inspection bay but do not touch the interior under any circumstances."

Mrs. Adams, who appeared to be at least eighty-five years old, was a well-dressed, sprightly woman who was most indignant at having to wait so long to have that 'nuisance', as she referred to the van, taken away. But there was nothing wrong with her eyesight, as it soon became obvious that she knew most of the comings and goings along Clermont Terrace. She accepted the officer's introductions as a matter of course seeming to pay little heed to their rank.

"I have lived here all of my married life, and every week the traffic gets heavier along this road," she complained. "Those men going up to London try to leave their cars along here but I get out in the mornings and point out the 'No Parking' signs. They can take their noisy machines somewhere else or learn to walk just like we used to," with that she sat back in her chair.

She had offered them a cup of tea but they had politely declined. Having let Mrs. Adams lodge her complaint Jones asked her what she knew about the van. According to the old lady she had first seen the van very early on the Monday morning of the previous week.

"Did you see who left it there?"

"No, I am usually in bed by ten and it wasn't there then but it has been there ever since. I have kept an eye on it but nobody has been near it. I want it moved!" she said, thumping her stick on the floor for emphasis.

Just then there was a heavy knock on the front door Smith looked out of the window, as Mrs. Adams went to answer her door.

"Oh it's the breakdown lorry," Smith said and he went to the door. He wanted to make sure the lorry driver knew what was wanted. Mrs. Adams came back into the room.

"Well it is about time that was done but I was thinking they don't usually send a Detective Inspector for a parked car do they?" she said looking hard at the Inspector.

Despite her years Mrs. Adams was still an insightful woman and had not missed the importance of the two officers. Jones felt that he owed her something so he explained that a black van had been linked to the death of a young man and as her van had been abandoned at about the same time they had to check to see if her van was the one they were looking for

"Oh that poor boy, I read about it in the paper such terrible things happening these days. Good job my William isn't still alive he would wonder what the world was coming to." She sat silent for a while looking over at a photo on her mantelpiece.

"Is that your husband?" asked Smith.

"Yes. He was a colonel in the Hussars and we spent quite a few years out in India but I was always glad to get home. William died ten years ago this November. I do miss him so."

Jones thanked her for assistance and told her that he would send a constable round to take an official statement. Mrs. Adam rose to see him out and all three stood on the pavement as the tow lorry and its load left. The officers thanked Mrs. Adams again and left.

In the car Smith suggested that they send young Masters down to the garage.

"He's mad on cars sir, and perhaps he can be of use down there on the van, or at the least he can see how they do the search?"

"Good idea," agreed Jones as they drove back into town." I think I will have a word with Masters myself as I have decided to get a small car."

"Well he's your man," said Smith.

When Jones returned to his office later that afternoon he found an urgent message to call Inspector MacDonald at the Yard. Luckily he was able to catch the Inspector just as he was leaving the office.

"What do we have John?" he asked his friend.

"It seems that there had been two incidents involving suspicious activities along the shoreline just outside Whitby," explained Mac Donald. "The first one was spotted by a patrolling constable, apparently two large crates were unloaded into a white van which then headed out towards London. The second was called in by a citizen walking his dog along the cliffs, again crates were unloaded this time into a black van. The man did get the license number so we are tracing it right now. Both boats were small with outboard motors most probably from a larger boat waiting out in International waters. "

"Interesting. I have a case of a very rich man disappearing, yet his empty boat was found floating between Portsmouth and the Isle of Wight. Just wondering out loud if there could be a connection. Is there much activity going on in this area lately?"

"Unfortunately there is always smuggling going on along the South Coast, too many inlets and not enough men to police. But usually they are small affairs, but I will send out feelers when I send out the memos with details of the latest landings and will follow up ASAP with license numbers. In the meantime spread the word around your group and let me know if you learn any more. Thanks Dai"

Hurriedly Jones wrote out a memo to each of his colleagues in the Network explaining what had happened and telling them to be on the lookout for any sudden increase in the drug trade in their area. Jones took his memo to the desk Sgt for immediate circulation in Kent and Hampshire as well as Sussex.

Meeting Smith in the corridor Jones asked him what news there was from Rottingdean.

"The Sgt knew of several residents who have collections of antiques, three of whom lived in big houses a little out of the village. But the Sgt's daughter has a friend called Rosie who cleans at a big house and she has often spoken of the number of collections of pretty stuff where she works".

"Do we know which house that is?"

"Yes the Sgt says it is the house just below the windmill. It is owned by a Mr. Moore." Jones drew a deep breath.

"Does the Sgt know this man?"

"He has seen him around the village, mostly at the weekends as apparently Moore spends at least three days a week at his business in London."

"And what is that business?"

"Nobody knows sir," answered Smith.

"I'll add his name to our list. You know Jack I'm wondering if this is the Mr. Moore that I met at that community meeting, if so I'm afraid he is a nasty piece of work," Jones said, as he wrote Moore's name on his pad. "Is there any family?"

"Yes there are two young children, but Moore is a widower. There is a live- in housekeeper, a Mrs. Stevens and a live-in nanny, a Miss Blake. That is all we know about him," finished up Smith.

"We'll go and see him. Find out what days he goes to London and we will pay a surprise visit on one of his home days. Arrange that as soon as possible please. Let's see if we can find out if it was his house that Bobby hit."

"What about the Whitehawk boys any luck yet?"

"Yes we know the brother and sister. Their name is Knowles and they live near the top of Freshfield Road. The boy does have a juvenile record with us a couple of 'bound overs' to keep the peace, and a fine for assaulting another boy."

"What about the girl?"

"Nothing as yet but she is known simply because she follows her brother about."

"Do they work?"

"No the boy is waiting to go into the army and the sister apparently just hangs around home."

"Parents?"

"Just a mother. They're Londoners, had to leave London suddenly and came down here to live with a sister. She kicked them out when she had more children of her own that left Mrs. Knowles with nowhere to live. The council were forced to house them in Whitehawk"

"Where's the father?"

"Doesn't appear to be one sir" answered Smith.

"How about the other boys?"

"Constable Masters is up in the area now and we should have all addresses in full by the end of today."

"Good. Change of plan, let's get them all interviewed tomorrow. At their homes. That way they cannot warn each other. Do you have enough people for that?"

"Yes."

"You and I will do the Knowles family. Are any of the gang members under sixteen do we know?"

"I'll make sure of their ages before we go in. At least we know the Knowles kids are older."

Jones's team were gathered in the conference room by eight-thirty Tuesday morning. It had been a week since the last team briefing and Jones was anxious that each of the officers was up to date. He knew that the impending interviews with the young people should provide the impetus to get Bobby's murder solved but they had to be conducted with skill to encourage the kids to speak freely.

Jones sat back while Sgt Smith ran through each of the pertinent items to date; the approximate time of the murder, the discovery of the body, the abandoned black van, the alleged robbery, the enmity between the two groups of youths, the money found in Bobby's box and Bobby's missing car. He waited for questions. One officer asked if Moore's house had been visited yet. Smith answered

"Later this week." A second officer said that he had dealt with Bobby and his friends on a couple of occasions but nothing major, just moving them along when they were hanging around outside the Black Swan.

"A bit cheeky, but nothing more," he remarked.

Smith went to his notes, "The Inspector and myself will go to see the Knowles brother and sister. Det. Constable Masters and W.P.C. Jenkins will visit Steven Chase and Andrew Ball, and Sgt Handley and W.P.C. Mills from Uniform will visit Raymond Brice and Alice Baker. Now" added Smith raising his voice over the murmur, "reminders to check the ages of each person before you begin and if the parents are there invite them to sit in. But remember if the kids are over sixteen it is their choice whether or not the parents sit in. After completing the interviews, write up your notes quickly. Let the Inspector or I know immediately if anything vital comes out of your interview. Remember to take a photo of Bobby with you."

"Right," said Jones taking over. "Today's interviews are very important both for what information we can gain from these kids and how we can build on those facts."

As the group began to stir he called out,

"Remember that Bobby Williams was beaten to death, a savage, violent attack on a young man. The perpetrator could be equally young, but strong and very determined. Look at the hands and faces for bruises or any kind of sign of being in a fight. Good luck."

Driving up to Whitehawk Smith took the opportunity to explain to Jones the origins of the area which was originally a downland valley called Whitehawk Bottom. There was little housing other than the very small manor farm. In the early 1930's Brighton Council chose this area as the new estate for the people made homeless due to the slum clearance that occurred in East Brighton and parts of Kemp Town. Unfortunately because of the isolation from the main part of the town, and the occupant's lack of both education and trade experience, the residents of the new council community were either unemployed or earned very low wages. The area, in part due to its proximity with the Racecourse, became a refuge for small time crooks and soon gained a reputation of being lawless. The isolation from the main part of town did not help matters, consequently the area was shunned by the majority of town folk and the entire area gradually became another slum.

As they walked up the short path to the Knowles' front door the men's ears were assailed by a tremendous blast of music coming from an upstairs open windows .Jones second knock was answered by a woman, perhaps in her late thirties, blonde and very attractive.

"Are you Mrs. Knowles?' asked Smith as he introduced himself and Jones.

"Yes. What's this all about? I suppose our Tommy has been in trouble again." she said angrily, Jones thought she was obviously used to policemen knocking on her door. "Just to confirm that you are the mother of Tom and Maggie Knowles.,"

"Yes, yes, what do yer want?" she asked leading them into the house. Although not offered, Jones took a seat in the small front room.

"We are here to speak to both Tom and Maggie about certain events. Please call them down. My Sgt and I did see faces upstairs so we know they are here."

Smith moved across to the foot of the stairs as Mrs. Knowles shouted upstairs. After a minute or two, heavy boots clumped their way down the stairs. First to appear was the boy. A tall, thin young man with bleached long hair and a cigarette dangling from the corner of his mouth sauntered down the stairs. Behind him came the younger sister, shorter, with black curly hair, long earrings, lots of makeup and continually chewing gum, American style.

Ignoring the officers Tom leaned indolently against the hall wall, hands in pockets, legs crossed at the ankles.

"What's up mum, what are these two rozzers doing 'ere?" Tom continued to ignore the men and just looked at his mother for a response.

Smith stood up, walked across to Tom and said quietly "This gentleman is Detective Inspector Jones and I am Detective Sergeant Smith and we are here to speak to both you and your sister regarding the death of Bobby Williams. Now sit down." While Maggie looked stunned Tom seemed more frightened than shocked as he slid into an armchair.

Smith again, "How old are you?"

Tom answered, "I'm seventeen and Maggie is sixteen."

Smith continued, "Under the law it is not necessary for parents to be present at police interviews if the subject of the interview is over sixteen years of age." Smith looked as Tom and Maggie looked at each other than both nodded,

"Mum can stay," said Tom "but Maggie and me don't know nuffink about Bobby's death."

"But you both knew Bobby, is that correct?"

"Yes."

"And were you friends?"

"No."

“Were you enemies?” The kids looked at their mother who was finding it very difficult to stay out of the conversation.

“It were just silly little childish things. All of them would fight whenever they met up anywhere, Tommy told me that,” she said turning to the officers. ”Just kids’ stuff.”

“Do you have a job?” asked Jones looking at both of them. Mum answered for them.

“Yes Maggie just started training at a hairdresser’s and Tom, well no point in him getting anything steady, he’ll be going into the Service soon”.

“Tell me more about your run-ins with Bobby and his friends,” asked Smith. The two then told of the arguments and fights the two groups had had in the past. The meetings at the park, down near the local shops, at the Level and at the Roller Rink on the seafront.

Did you ever personally threaten Bobby?” asked Jones sternly. By now Tom had lost his swagger, he was pale and looking rather nauseous.

“Tom?” his mother was puzzled by his reluctance to answer the question. Then Tom burst into tears.

“I didn’t mean anyfink by it. I thought I could frighten Bobby and that girl Pam.”

“And why would you want to do that?” asked Smith as he stood up and moved across to Tom’s chair.

“Because, ‘cause I fancied that Pamela and she wouldn’t even give me a chance.”

“Bloody stuck up little bitch,” exploded Maggie “she caused all this problem, serves her right.”

“Oh Maggie how can you say that, the boy is dead,” Mrs. Knowles crossed the room and tried to calm her daughter but Maggie stomped off across to the doorway and stood there just looking at everyone.

“We have a few more questions. Do you have a regular meeting place? A sort of hangout where you all meet?”

“Yes,” said Tom “It’s the old barn up on the Racehill. We go there at least twice a week just to hang out.”

“When was the last time you were there?’

“We always go on Mondays so as we can talk about what we did on the weekend.”

Jones stood looking down at the cowed boy,

"Tom, did you get in a fight with Bobby Williams and kill him?"

Mrs. Knowles went to her son, "Tell the truth Tom, it could have been an accident."

"No mum, I didn't kill him. I ain't seen him since before he went to the soccer match in London, honest mum."

The two officers closed their notebooks and prepared to leave. They thanked Mrs. Knowles and then warned both Tom and Maggie that most probably they would be back to speak to them later that week and they were not to leave the area.

The old barn wasn't difficult to spot, going up Warren Road the building lay just down the hill on the north side.

"There might not be any connection at all with the William's boy but let's go and have a look around," suggested Jones.

Smith parked the car on the grass verge and the two men strode across the grass. From the outside it seemed that the only things holding up the roof were the four thick corner posts. The walls had more gaps than planks, the two windows were empty of glass and there were more tiles missing than present on the roof. Strangely the door was almost complete and swung open without any noise. Inside the floor area was covered in smelly damp straw and bits of rubbish such as bottles, chocolate bar wrappers, even old comics. The inside had originally been divided into two sections, perhaps for two horses. The dividing wall was solid and did provide both shelter and privacy from anybody walking by. In one of the sections the detectives found old wooden orange crates set up for seats, a couple even had old cushions on them. Full ashtrays sat on the floor between the boxes and a couple of large work size torches were laying on the cushions.

"Obviously their hangout," said Smith, "I'll collect some of these butts for examination." Smith pulled a couple of bags from his pocket and carefully emptied both ashtrays. Jones had wandered over into the other side.

"Anything there?" asked Smith.

"Not yet." Jones was poking around in the dirty straw. "Wait a minute. Jack stand back just there and take a look at the floor in this section. Tell me what you see." Smith moved back a few paces and carefully looked over the small area.

"The straw is all pushed up like somebody or something has been pushing at it. Perhaps a fight. Look at that damp spot." Smith pointed to a small patch in one corner.

"Yes I'd seen that. I'm going to take a small scrape of it for testing. I think its blood, maybe a few days old but definitely this is a blood stain. Both men moved deeper into the corners poking at the straw and knocking the wooden sides to see if anything was hidden. Just then Smith swore as he caught his foot on something on the floor.

"All right Sgt?" But Smith didn't answer he was examining a chunk of wood that he had dug out of the straw. "This is what tripped me. If I'm not mistaken this could be an old blood stain like the other one on the floor."

Quickly Jones took a look at the wood. "Get that back to the car. Wrap it carefully. I'll call the station and get a forensic team up here to search the place and I'll get a uniform up here quickly to secure it. Who is the closest constable for this area? Call him in to keep the place secure until the forensic team have finished." Once Smith had finished with the car 'phone he started to speculate on the day's progress.

"We have to be careful not to jump to any conclusions that this was where Bobby was killed or that the Whitehawk kids had anything to do with it. But if Tom and his pals did kill him then how did they get Bobby down to the building site? Tom doesn't have a car and I'm not sure that he can even drive. On the other hand Tom does strike me as a bully and has been had up before for beating other kids,"

Jones shifted position in his seat. "If the pathologist can make a match between either of the stains on the wood or the floor, with Bobby, that could give us the killing spot." He looked up, "Good here comes somebody." Masters and a second policeman strode across.

"I picked up your message Inspector so I drove over to pick up P.C. Thornton who was doing his beat halfway up Elm Grove. I thought that giving him a lift would be helpful sir."

"Well done son," said Smith and then walked Constable Thornton around the barn and explained what the Inspector wanted.

"All the interviews finished Masters?" asked Jones.

"Yes sir, the men are just typing up their reports, should be ready by the time we get back."

"Good. I hear that you have a good knowledge of cars, is that right?"

"Oh yes sir. That's my hobby tinkering with old engines and cars. I was checking out that black van when you called."

"Excellent. I want you to walk all over this ground and on up to the road to see if you can find any tracks at all that could have been made in the past few days. Make a cast of anything you find and take it down to the mechanics and see if anyone can identify them. Let me know if you find anything."

"Yes sir. I will," answered the young constable.

CHAPTER FOURTEEN

Moore had spent several days waiting for information and was growing angrier by the hour as none of his informants knew anybody who had the skills to open a safe like Moore's. But then he had a stroke of luck. That morning he had heard from a former contact who knew of an ex-soldier who had worked for Special Services during the final years of the war opening safes and even buildings.in France and then Germany, as the enemy retreated. Moore had sent Charlie down to the London Docks to get more information from the caller and now he was waiting for Charlie to check in. The telephone rang and Moore stopped pacing.

'It's me Charlie. The man's name is Dusty Miller. He never organized a job but always worked for others who had enough to pay for the best safe cracker in Europe. "

"Well he might be the best bloody safe cracker in the world but if he was in my house he's going to pay. Where does he live?"

"He doesn't have a street address but knows Miller lives in East Croydon and uses a pub called The Duke of Wellington near Bealuh Road."

"Description?"

"Average height, dark hair, balding, tattoos on his forearms, wiry but extremely strong. No family lives in digs somewhere near the pub."

"That's all?"

"Yes guv" Moore slammed down the phone .Now he had the safe cracker. He wasn't the organizer but he must have known something about the others to have agreed to take the job. Moore dialled a number, on the second ring a voice answered "Fred" Moore spoke softly into the phone giving all the information on Miller and instructions to have Miller found by that evening. "Call back when you have him for further instructions,"

Moore was feeling happier .soon he would have his package back. He knew that once word got around that Miller had been found and dealt with others would talk. Soon he would have the name of the third man and there would be absolutely no connection to himself. That's why he paid top money for enforcers.

Miller spent many evenings at his local pub, just around the corner from his lodgings. He had never married, worked infrequently and spent most of his spare time playing darts or cards at the Duke, or following his favourite horses at the several racetracks he could reach by bus or Underground. Dusty was an amiable man, very strong but never subscribed to physical violence to get what he wanted. He had stayed in the military as a career, was content with his life and wanted no more than to jog along like the thousands of other ex-soldiers who had adapted to civilian life. As Miller seldom paid any attention to what was in the newspaper other than the football scores or the racing results he had no idea that the young man on the Rottingdean job had been murdered, even if he had known his name.

There had been a spurt of building jobs available around Miller's area and in the past couple of days he had made friends with a younger man who had just taken a room nearby. He told Miller that he was employed by Hall's, who had won the contract to provide materials to construct the new roadway around Croydon. Fred, that is what he called himself, was of average height but sturdily built, with a mass of brown curly hair and like Dusty lived on his own and like Dusty, spent his evenings in the pub. Dusty enjoyed Fred's company and felt the younger man had the makings of a good darts player. They spent many hours just discussing football and horses while nursing their beer. Fred had asked Dusty to have supper with him one evening but Dusty was a very routine man. He cooked his own meals, always.

He once told a mate who was curious why Dusty wouldn't eat out. "I ate enough army rations and foreign food to last me a lifetime. Now I eat my own cooking and that's that."

"Do you ever go away from Croydon?" asked Fred.

"Oh I sometimes go to London to watch soccer "

Fred sat staring at his drink then 'Well I'm going down to Brighton this weekend why don't you come down with me?" Fred suggested "We can go to Sherry's find a couple of girls and have a good time dancing. You still like girls Dusty" Fred said with a sly wink at his friend. "Or we can go to the pubs. Lots of entertainment in Brighton .we could even do the pier now they have lots of new sideshows let's do it this Saturday .What you say Dusty, just you an' me then we'd have a good time just the two of us." But Dusty was not to be persuaded. He was not keen to return to Brighton and how could he tell his new friend about the robbery. He would be shocked. Later in the evening Fred tried to interest Dusty again in going to Brighton.

"Oh leave it will yer. I aint going with you. Go by yourself. You're younger than me. Brighton on a Saturday night is just up your street. Go on, push off". Fred went over to talk to two other men at the bar and later Dusty saw him leave. When Dusty left the pub at closing time Fred was waiting outside.

"I thought you'd gone 'ome," said Dusty.

"Naaw. I went to telephone my brother-in-law. He often runs a poker game, strictly illegal of course, in the basement of one of the big hotels on the seafront, 'e works there so has the run of the basement and no one troubles 'im. You told me you like a good game of poker. I've been down there before and I know all the players. Interested?'" Now this was much more attractive to Dusty as he was an excellent poker player and loved a game with good players.

"I'll let you know at the pub tomorrow lunch time." Dusty couldn't help thinking that he would really enjoy a game with some new players.

Dusty worked out that if he took a taxi from the station straight to the hotel and then back again he would be okay. Dusty was always very cautious about revisiting an area where he had recently done a job. But in a taxi he would never be out on the streets. Finally Dusty agreed and told Fred the next day when they met over the lunchtime beer. They arranged to meet at the station and catch the six-thirty five down to Brighton.

While Fred had been softening up Dusty ready for the showdown his partner had always been in the vicinity keeping a low profile. Being such a physically large man he didn't wish to arouse Dusty's suspicions so he never went to the pub nor hung around Dusty's digs. He and Fred met each day in a café on the other side of town to pass on further instructions from Moore and then to firm up their plan. Unexpectedly Moore had a crisis with his 'other' business interests and had already given the large man specific instructions on how they were to deal with Miller.

At six- twenty, as Fred waited for Dusty at the bottom of the steps leading to the platform, his partner was sitting on a bench a little further down the platform. To the ordinary observer there was nothing to connect Fred and the large man on the bench but as soon as Fred saw Dusty coming down thc stcps hc signalled and the large man stepped behind a billboard out of Miller's view.

Within a few minutes the train pulled in and Fred quickly led Dusty to a compartment almost at the end of the train. Fred needed a non-corridor carriage, which suited Dusty as he had no wish to be with others. But no sooner had Dusty sat down than the door opened and this very large, aggressive looking man stepped up into the compartment.

"Hey!" said Dusty "this is taken go find your own compartment." Dusty turned to Fred for help but Fred was sitting quietly in the corner reading his newspaper. Dusty was angry, wondering why Fred hadn't helped him with this man and gave Fred a hard look. Fred didn't take any notice instead asking Dusty if he had bought enough money for the game. By then the train was moving and Dusty knew he had to accept the situation at least until the next station. Soon after leaving the station the intruder got up and pulled all the window blinds down on the platform side.

"What do you 'fink yer doing then?" shouted Dusty immediately jumping up from his seat and looking at Fred for support and becoming increasingly angry at Fred's passive response towards the stranger's oafish behaviour. It was then that Dusty's new friend decided to help out. Fred stood up smiled at Dusty then turned to the large man and calmly said

"All set then?' while he swiftly turned back and hit Dusty viciously across the face.

"What's that for?" screamed Dusty falling back onto his seat.

"For the Rottingdean job, and that's what this is for," said Fred, again striking Dusty across the head. Dusty was terrified; he was trapped in this compartment with these two animals and had no hope of escape until the next station. Despite the limited space in the compartment the large man pulled Dusty off his seat dumped him on the floor and began stomping on him with his heavy boots.

"Christ, just tell me what yer want to know?" begged Dusty trying to shield his head. "Give me a chance an' I'll tell yer".

By now Dusty was bleeding from cuts on his head and doubled up from the numerous blows to his chest and abdomen. The train had come to a stop at Haywards Heath station but while Fred sat on Dusty the large man pulled down the door window and leaned outside, effectively preventing anybody from getting into their compartment. The train started again. Fred sat back on the seat. Dusty was still on the floor in between the seats coughing and moaning and the large man was standing grinning at the door.

Fred leaned down into Dusty's face and said "Okay tell us what you know, you have two minutes."

In a breaking voice Dusty began. "There was a kid who did the driving, 'e stayed downstairs all the time. The other man was with me in the bedroom with the safe."

"What about the package from the safe?" asked Fred bending Dusty's arm until it threatened to snap.

"He took the package to London, the next day. 'e was to hand it over there."

"Who to?"

"I dunno- I don't fink he knew 'oo it was. None of us knew whose house it was, not the real name."

"What was in the package?" several more kicks landed before Dusty was able to answer.

"We never looked. We was tol' not to."

Dusty lay on the floor between the bench seats. He was bleeding badly from the back of his head and his nose. His breathing was shallow and he had vomited over his trousers. Fred checked his watch and looked at his partner. They knew that within minutes the train would be entering Clayton Tunnel.

It was there at the north entrance that they planned to throw Miller out. Fred pulled down the window and looked out to the front of the train and nodded to his partner. More kicks landed on Dusty and then he was hauled screaming off the floor across to the open window, Dusty knew the train route as well as anyone and was terrified as the driver blew the whistle for the approaching tunnel.

He struggled and kicked out as they bundled him out of the window vainly he clung to the wooden sashes of the window frame but soon he was out the window and the two thugs heard the clunk as Dusty met his end against the tunnel entrance.

Napier had settled into his new flat in Hove. Although still not able to get a legitimate job he was very reluctant to move away from the South. The air was clean, salty but clean, there was lots of green space around to walk and explore that was easily accessible by public transport. He had found in Brighton a town that was always busy, from the noisy holidaymakers enjoying the variety of attractions along the seafront and on the Piers, to the more upscale thriving businesses and shopping area behind the seafront hotels. From Little Preston Street in the west to the top end of St. James's Street in the east there were shops, restaurants, cafes, diners, pubs, theatres, banks and even an Aquarium. He enjoyed delving into the history of the area checking out the notable buildings such as the Royal Pavilion, The Dome, the Public Library, and the Regency architecture, Preston Manor and several Art Galleries and Museums. At the other end of the scale Napier was well aware that Brighton had an underbelly of dodgy activities, those that attracted London folk although Napier chose not to socialize in those circles and his move to Hove was his way of separating his personal life from that of his business activities.

To enable him to move Napier had done a couple more jobs since Moore's house while constantly looking for that legitimate financial position, .Consequently Napier had not seen the original news of an unidentified body being found on a building site. It was only when he was catching up on some back editions of the Argus that he learned the body was that of young Bobby. Napier was shocked that Bobby was dead and his first thoughts were that Bobby had been in an accident. The idea that his death was related in any way to the Rottingdean job simply didn't occur to Napier. But a later edition had stated that William's death was now a murder investigation... Still Napier felt quite secure that the job and Bobby's murder were unrelated. He knew that the Boss abhorred violence and as Napier hadn't heard anything since the meeting in

London he felt that the Boss was satisfied. But the more he thought about Bobby's death the more unsettled he became.

For a week Napier stewed about what to do, he didn't go out much and had lost his appetite, simply unable to shake his fears; recently he'd received an invitation from his cousin to visit her, her husband to meet their new baby. His cousin lived in Looe, a small fishing village in Devon; He ignored her letter at first being so frightened to leave his flat, let alone get on a train. He walked to and fro, to and fro trying vainly to work out an escape plan.

"What can I do? Somebody is after me. I don't know who or why but they are out there!" he stopped. Abruptly he turned and headed for his bedroom

"Enough already!" he yelled at the walls. "If the bastards want me they'll have to find me first!"

Hurriedly packing a small suitcase, he locked up and left a note for his landlady. He knew there was a train down to Southampton in an hour but he needed to see someone first.

Napier had met Jim one evening in his local pub. They were each sitting alone nursing a pint when Jim decided that Napier looked like somebody he once met at the army barracks in Aldershot. Napier had never been to Aldershot but as Jim seemed to be a friendly man with a multitude of amusing stories they had struck up a friendship. Although they had exchanged names neither man knew precisely where the other lived or what they did for money. It really didn't seem important as they met only at the pub and enjoyed each other's company.

Jim was sitting at a back table when Napier almost threw himself through the pub door.

"Ay mate you're in a rush, what's up, going somewhere? Time for a quick pint?"

"No thanks Jim, Can't stop. I'm in a hurry." Napier moved the seat closer to his friend.

"Look I'm going away for a couple of months. Can't tell you where or why but if anybody asks for me please, please tell them that you don't know anything!"

"But why? You in some kind of trouble?"|

"Yes and No."

“Well I need something in case of an emergency. What about where you’re working?”

“I don’t know what I’ll be doing. I just need to get away.” Looking at his watch Napier stood up ready to leave.

“Look I’ll give you the name of the little café near where I’ll be but only tell in case of dire emergency. I‘m trusting you Jim, with my life!” With that Napier left the pub, walked quickly around to Hove station. Bought a ticket for Southampton and within minutes was on the train heading west.

CHAPTER FIFTEEN

It was Thursday afternoon and Jones was updating his Super about the smugglings.

"These crooks go to ground so quickly. No doubt the drugs were already being cut before breakfast the same morning that the vans were spotted," he had said.

"What about Customs and Excise do they know anything?" asked the Super.

"Mac said he'd sent his men into the nearby marinas to check with the Harbourmaster for any unusual activities but they said they could account for every boat that belonged there. So that was it."

"What's next then?"

"I do have a couple of ideas and if it's okay with you I would like to go and see Mac next week to discuss them."

"Should I know beforehand?"

"I would rather keep them to myself for now Sir, they might not even be feasible."

"Okay but I need to know what is going on."

"Right sir." said Jones and hurried down the corridor to his own office where he knew Smith was waiting hopefully with a report from forensics.

The interviews with the other members of the Knowles group hadn't provided any new information on the Williams' case. Each of the interviewing officers felt that Tom and Maggie were the definite leaders and organizers and the other four kids were simply hangers on. Yet Jones felt certain that there was a connection between Bobby, Tom and the barn on the hill but so far they had not found a concrete link.

The search of the black van had not yielded any prints at all, every surface had been wiped clean which was surprising but convinced Jones that he had the right vehicle. Officers had been able to track down a couple of the former owners of the van but each owner had a Bill of Sale to the next owner, with the final owner admitting that the van had been stolen about eighteen months ago and was able to show the insurance claim for compensation.

The second car that Jones wanted found, Bobby's Hillman, was discovered out on the Steyning Road, behind the cement works. A local citizen had called in at Shoreham sub-station to say that the car had been sitting around in the back parking area for almost two weeks. He had noticed it from the top of the cliffs when he took his morning walk past the factory. The local sergeant thought that it wouldn't do any harm to let it sit for a few more days in case the owner was on holiday or something. But as soon as he read Smith's memo the officer at Shoreham had the car towed into Brighton. So far forensic was unable to find any clues other than those leading to Bobby.

Nothing was adding up on this case, Jones was finding it extremely difficult to get two clues that linked together and his frustration was beginning to show as daily he grew more impatient with the lack of any real progress.

The office door opened suddenly and Smith walked in carrying a brown envelope.

"Just picked this up from the desk sir, just in, from Marshall," said Smith as he handed the envelope to Jones.

"Good, at last, now we shall see," muttered Jones as he tore open the letter.

"Oh, that's disappointing the patch on the floor was old animal blood." He read further, he looked up at Smith

"But the blood on the block of wood matches that of Bobby. The pathologist had taken a sample of Bobby's blood the evening he was found." Jones sat back in his chair, "So Bobby was in that barn and was hit with that piece of wood." He thought for a while and then standing up said, "Get the Knowles, Tom, Maggie and Missus down here for tomorrow afternoon at three o'clock. Let them know today, that a car will pick them up at two-thirty prompt. We'll let that boy stew for a night and then we'll see what he has to say." Jones turned to Smith "What do you think Sgt? Do we have the killer?" Sgt Smith took a few minutes before answering the question.

"Maybe, but we still haven't figured out how they got Bobby's body down to The Level and we cannot connect them to the black van. We don't even know if that van is connected to the Williams' case. It's all a bit dodgy at present isn't it sir? Even the chunk of wood could be older than we think and have nothing to do with this event."

"Come on Smith, you know that we're obliged to follow up with the kids, but I have to agree with you that there are too many questions and not enough answers. Anything we have is almost coincidental to the murder. We have to be moving closer to the solution but as yet there are so many parts missing that I can't begin to see a complete picture." Jones sat for a moment watching the rain clouds moving quickly across the heavy sky." I so wanted to have this case wrapped up before the funeral tomorrow but that's not going to happen. Damn it."

"We have the other men in the station for re-interviewing about the robberies, how you want to handle that?"

"I think I'll ask Inspector Stanley to do these. Being from London he's very familiar with the London gangs and perhaps he can pick up on why these men are working down here. I have shared all our notes with him including the latest one so perhaps he can get something more out of these men. Are you okay with that Jack?"

"Oh yes sounds like a good idea to me."

"Are they all here?"

"We have Spenser and Maitland, they are older lags. I also called in young Binder, if you remember he did have quite a solid alibi for each of the robberies but he was so scared of something he could hardly talk. I want to see if he is frightened enough to let out what he knows."

"Okay sounds good. But there was one more person. He went missing if I remember."

"Yes Masters is still tracking down Mr. Hillier.

"Okay we'll pass that information to Stanley. Now about tomorrow. Bobby's funeral at eleven, a visit to Moore at one o'clock." Jones looked up

"I find it very strange that we have never received a report of a robbery at any house that night. Yet Bobby's friend Pamela said that Bobby had told her he had done the job that night. Hmmm Anyway then we'll be back in time for the Knowles at three o'clock. Tomorrow could be a very interesting day!"

CHAPTER SIXTEEN

It was an early start for Jones as he wanted to catch up with events at the Greyhound track. Before leaving for the funeral. The track's solicitor and manager had agreed to be at his office by 8.30 and they were prompt. As Smith joined them the solicitor, Sackville-Smythe began,

"Since we last met I have made many enquiries about our missing Mr Forest and this is a summary from those findings," he said handing the three men several sheets. "As you can see despite making many telephone calls and personal visits to the appropriate people we were unable to learn anything new about Forest's background. We know he arrived here about three years ago from South Africa. We did learn from others that he was friendly, polite and enjoyed spreading his money about. By sending my assistant, with a letter of introduction, to the manager of each bank in his neighbourhood. I did find out where he banked. There is no mortgage on any of his five houses, or any debts on his boats or his seven antique cars."

"What about income. Wasn't the bank curious about where he got his money?" asked Jones.

"Yes Inspector but as he regularly transfers money from the Bank of Transvaal and, according to that manager, they have no reason to think there is anything illegal about his business... I did ask about ownership of the dogs, but his bank manager had no record of those transactions," finished the solicitor.

"So to sum up we have a missing wealthy man of whom little is really known, an empty yacht floating in the Channel. No sign of him living at any of his properties. A man who has a regular income from South Africa and has, or had six pedigree greyhounds."

"Don't forget the money missing from my accounts," interrupted the track manager.

"Of course," replied Jones. "What do you find Sackville-Smyth?"

"Well Inspector I find the whole thing rather bizarre, especially as he has no known relatives, or heirs to his money or possessions. I would speculate that he is dead whether accidently or otherwise. Or he is involved in something that has become so dangerous that he has been forced to disappear. What is our next step Inspector?"

"I have been thinking about this case, especially the abandoned yacht, The Hampshire police they will start at the Harbour Master's office, where the boat is berthed, work backwards to track the movements of the boat."

"Anything else for me?" asked the solicitor.

"Just keep me informed if you learn anything more about Forest.

"What about the missing money?" persisted the racetrack manger?

"I would suggest you have your solicitor find you a good forensic accountant to go over your books and track down the missing money. Perhaps the dogs and the missing money are unrelated, but until we find out about the money, and the man we'll not know the relationship. Good day gentlemen, thanks for coming in and I will keep you informed.''

"Do you know Jack" said Jones after the others had left," I have a funny feeling that our missing man could be connected to the diamond smuggling that is going on along our coast.

"Anything concrete?"

"No just a gut feeling!"

It was a beautiful October day as the men drove up Elm Grove to the church. The sky was a clear blue and the trees still had some summer leaves dangling from their branches.

"Not the kind of day one thinks of when burying a young man is it?" remarked Smith. Jones nodded.

The church was set back from the road as the men joined the procession of mourners slowly proceeding to the church doors... The officers sat at the back, not wanting to intrude on the family's grief yet letting their presence remind the gathering that Bobby's violent death was still an active investigation. Neither of the officers expected to learn anything from the congregation but it was always interesting to see who attended. Both Smith and Jones were well aware that sometimes, just sometimes, the killer would be at his victim's funeral, some macabre delight in seeing the pain that their actions had caused.

As the organist bought his very sombre selection to a close the low murmurs stopped and the congregation stood as the vestry door opened. Mr. Williams led his wife and the two eldest of their daughters into the front pew, almost in arm's reach of the coffin. Behind the Williams, Pamela and her mother walked followed by various relatives. Jones had noticed that Bobby's other friends were present, mostly standing with their mothers. Smith nudged Jones and indicated a group across from them. Mrs. Knowles, Tom and Maggie were standing at the back. As the service progressed it became obvious, by the turning of heads that the policeman had been recognized and word had passed around the congregation.

As Jones listened to the minister speaking of Bobby's youth and the sobbing of family and friends became more pronounced, he became very angry at the injustice of life. He recalled his father's and grandfather's sudden death in the mine, and Stan's quick and violent death while doing his duty and now he was attending another violent death of an even younger man. He was very aware that Bobby had chosen his colleagues unwisely, that he had made poor decisions, but he didn't deserve to be dumped and left to die amongst the rubble. Jones promised himself there and then, in the church, that he would not abandon the memory of Bobby, that he would do whatever it took to bring the killers to justice.

After the coffin had been placed in the hearse ready for Bobby's final journey to the cemetery the policemen moved across to shake hands with Mr. and Mrs. Williams to offer further condolences, but declined to join them later for the standard refreshments. As the two officers passed the Knowles family, they acknowledged Mrs. Knowles by raising their hats but ignored the two young people who were shuffling around in the gritty path not daring to meet the eyes of the policemen. Others stopped the officers as they moved towards their car, curious to know how the investigation was going. The officers repeated to each inquiry that things were moving along slowly and then quickly left the area.

Jones' knowledge of Rottingdean was very scant so Smith took the opportunity, as they ate lunch, to explain the history of the village.

"It's recorded history," said Smith "goes back as far as the Domesday Book which records that the land of this small rural community was given to the Lord of Lewes for his assistance during the Battle of Hastings (1066)... Later on it became an artist's colony. But it wasn't until the coastal road between the village and Brighton was improved that the village started to develop as we know it today," explained Smith.

"What sort of people live here now?" Jones asked.

"On one level there are the old established families who can tell you exactly how far back their ancestors lived here. Then there are the so-called nouveau-riche who moved here during Victorian times and then of course there are a few who came down during the war. They had enough money to come and sit out the war in this quiet little backwater. Then there's the ordinary folk, the shopkeepers, the garage owners, small business people. So there is quite a mix really and like many villages there is a social separation between those with and those without money or even pedigree ancestors. These days it is considered, by those who are social climbers, to be a very chic place to live"

The local sergeant accompanied them to Moore's house confirming that he had stationed a constable to watch Moore and was to report if he left the house. Within the last half-hour the constable had reported that both Moore and the housekeeper were still in the house although the nanny and the young boy had left and had walked across to the Pond. A very solid looking woman answered the door and invited them in, asking them to wait a moment while she went to get Mr. Moore. It was obvious from the interior decorations that Moore had money. There was large antique statuary in the front hall as well as on the staircase. The walls were covered by large oil paintings and hanging on the wall at the top of the wide staircase Jones could see beautiful floor to ceiling tapestries. Two men strode across the hall.

"Inspector, this is my solicitor Mr. Saville-Smythe."

"Yes we met earlier today... This is Sgt Smith," replied Jones.

"Please go through to the drawing room, just through there to the left." Moore and his solicitor followed as the officers made their way into a large, beautifully furnished drawing room. The silk-covered settee, the yellow velvet floor to ceiling curtains and the highly polished mahogany tables continued the theme of wealth. When Moore joined both officers they showed him their warrant cards...

"Why are you here today?" he asked.

Jones took the lead, “Information has come our way that there was a robbery in this area about two weeks ago and we are asking local residents if they were aware of this.”

Moore replied that he had no knowledge of such an event and even called in his housekeeper to see if she had heard anything.

“No Mr. Moore. Neither me nor Rosie or Miss Blake have heard of anything like that.”

“Mr. Moore could you tell me exactly who lives in this house and what they do here?”

“Why we have just stated that we know nothing about a robbery?” demanded Moore.

”Well I suppose I can ask the locals. “ Moore quickly interrupted. “I don’t like people talking about my business but I suppose names and jobs are not much.”

A couple of times Jones asked him to slow down as he, wanted to ensure that his notes were factually correct. Smith hid a smile, he had quickly learned that whenever the Inspector felt that he was being lied to he began a deliberate strategy of provoking that person and now with the slow, methodical note-writing Jones had deliberately set about to annoy Moore.

“I wonder if Mrs. Stevens could make us a cup of tea I know my Sergeant could do with one?”

“Yes, yes. I should have offered before,” Moore said as he pulled the bell pull to summon Mrs. Stevens. “Please get tea for us Mrs Stevens”

“I’ll come with you if you don’t mind, I need a smoke,” Smith said as he purposefully strode across behind Mrs. Stevens. Moore was going to object but after looking at Jones’ face decided not to interfere

“I see that you have many antiques in your home. Have you checked them lately to confirm that nothing is missing?”

“I have a very modern alarm system installed to protect my possessions. So I see no need to be constantly checking everything. Besides Mrs. Stevens would inform me very quickly should she feel that something is missing,” was the very curt answer.

“Are antiques part of your business dealings?” asked Jones.

“No I deal mostly in small machines and tools.”

Jones suddenly stood and walked over to a small table that held a collection of snuffboxes.

"This is a very fine collection," he turned to Moore, "my mother collects small antique pieces similar to this but her collection cannot compare to yours. Do you buy your antiques locally in Sussex or in London?" Moore was surprised at the question and looked very hard at Jones.

"I have dealers looking for pieces all over the country," he answered sharply. "Although I fail to see what my antique collection and my business dealings have to do with anything," he added sharply. Jones knew that Moore was torn between showing the aggressive and rude tone he had taken at their previous meeting or whether to play the cooperative patient, wealthy man although of average height, Jones was well aware that Moore's snobbish demeanour barely concealed the toughness of a street fighter.

"Where is your office?" continued Jones.

"I do most of my business from an office in London."

"Well just to complete my notes please give me the address of your office and any other London numbers where I can get hold of you."

"Are you charging me with something?" Moore asked, very heatedly. By now he had moved to the edge of his chair and was becoming more agitated by the minute.

"Oh no, Mr. Moore, nothing like that. With possessions like you have we like to know how to contact you should anything happen. Remember that was the very important concern voiced at the meeting we both attended last week, local robberies, "finished Jones.

. The silence in the room became oppressive as Moore got up and began to look out of the windows.

"Do you have dealings with anybody else in Brighton other than antique dealers and your solicitor?" asked Jones. Still looking out of the window Moore answered that he used the established firm of Wilson, Buxton and Smythe, from Brunswick Terrace and reminded Jones that he had just met Saville-Smythe. By the time Jones had finished writing this information in his notebook Mrs. Stevens had brought in the tea tray and left again, perhaps to keep an eye on the policeman who was still in her kitchen.

As Moore poured tea Jones continued to look around the room, he was genuinely interested in antiques and he complimented Moore on the collection of sterling silver thimbles that he had spotted on another small table. While wandering around the room looking at various items he asked Moore why he chose to live in this village yet worked in London.

"My wife died when the children were very young and I simply couldn't stay in our London house any longer. I had heard about this small village from associates and with its proximity to Roedean, where my daughter attends, and the good rail service, it seemed an ideal place for us to start again."

"It certainly is handy for London," agreed Jones, "do you go by car or by train?'

"Mostly by train as my office is not too far away from Victoria station." Smith appeared at the drawing room door.

"My first smoke today."

With that comment both officers made a move to leave. Thanking Mr. Moore for his help and Mrs. Stevens for the tea they walked out of the front room into the hall. But Jones turned suddenly.

"Do you have a safe Mr. Moore?" Moore quickly said that he had one in his London office a floor model but nothing here at his home.

As the officers climbed into their car and left Jones saw that Moore was still standing in the doorway looking very puzzled and hopefully, thought Jones, feeling just a little more insecure than he was when they arrived.

"Nasty piece of work, that," remarked Smith. Jones agreed and then turned to Smith saying, "I didn't know you smoked?"

"I don't, but I always keep a pack in my pocket. You never know when they come in handy." Smith chuckled as he looked sideways at his boss. The local Sgt had decided to walk back down into the village so Smith and Jones headed back to Bartholomew Square along the coast road.

"How about you, what did Mrs. Stevens have to say?" Smith then relayed his conversation with Mrs. Stevens.

"I asked her if she had heard anything down at the shops about a robbery in the village but she hadn't heard anyone mention a robbery. Then I asked her if there was anything missing from Moore's house."

Smith looked across at Jones, "she said that it was funny I should mention that as a couple of weeks ago she had noticed that four snuffboxes were missing from the collection. She said she told Mr. Moore, but he had assured her that he had taken them to London for evaluation. Two have come back but not the others."

CHAPTER SEVENTEEN

The Knowles family was waiting in the lobby of the station, seated on the long narrow benches and looking very uncomfortable knowing that everyone could see them. Jones looked at them, spoke to the desk sergeant and then walked on down the corridor. Smith hung around chatting to the sergeant until he saw a signal to take the Knowles down to the interview room.

Mrs. Knowles was anxious to say something, "We went to the funeral today because I said we should. My kids didn't kill the boy, they aren't bad kids, they both miss their dad, I just know that and 'though they weren't the best of friends they had known Bobby for quite a while. I just felt we had to go and pay our respects to his family," she said collapsing in tears. This outburst took Jones by surprise and for a few moments he hesitated.

"Good turnout," said Smith. Mrs. Knowles nodded into her handkerchief. The two youngsters sat either side of their mother. Both were slumped down in their seats, eyes on the floor and looking scared.

Jones began "We have found new evidence regarding Bobby's murder and it doesn't look very good for you." he said, looking straight at Tom and Maggie. "We searched your hangout, the old horse barn up on the Racehill and we came away with several interesting items." He paused and looked at the two who were now very pale. Maggie was having some difficulty staying upright in her seat and was holding on tightly to the sides. Tom had maintained some composure and was attempting to stay calm by nonchalantly, looking out of the window.

"What did you find?" asked a very frightened Mrs. Knowles.

Jones opened his desk drawer and pulled out a cellophane wrapped chunk of wood. He remained silent for a few minutes watching the faces of the young people

"This was found in the barn amongst the straw in one corner of the divided section." Pushing the wood closer to the youngsters Jones continued, "As you can see this wood has stains on it. Blood stains. According to our forensic team the blood on this wood is identical to the blood taken as a sample from Bobby William's body. Therefore Bobby Williams was present in that barn shortly before his death."

There was a deathly hush in the room and then Tom stood up and shouted. "That's muffin to do with us Bobby was never in our place when we was there. I didn't kill him, neither did Maggie nor any of our gang. We'd never do that. Someone else had to have done it." Maggie had slid even further down in her seat and folded her arms as if in protection from these events. Jones looked at Maggie. She shook her head, "Nope I would never do summit like that. Neither me or Tom would do that."

Jones waited silently and patiently to see if the two had anything else but instead there was a discreet knock on the door. Smith opened it just a little way, protested to the caller that the Inspector was busy but listened to the message and then walked over to Jones. After hearing what his sergeant had to say, Jones announced that he had been called away for a few minutes. He told the family to wait there for his return. Det. Constable Masters and W.P.C. Jenkins would stay with them. Smith and Jones huddled together talking, as they went across to Smith's office. Inside they found a boy and a man waiting with the desk sergeant. Smith took the lead.

"How can we help you?" he asked the man.

"My name is Alan Brice and this is my son Andrew. Andrew is part of the Knowles gang, as you already know, and goes up to the old barn with them." Both Jones and Smith looked at the boy. Mr. Brice continued, "I told him never to mix with those two because they been trouble ever since they moved in, but no he never listens to me or his mum. But now he's done it." He shook his son by the shoulder, "Tell them." he ordered.

Andrew Brice was the youngest of the gang and the smallest. With his eyes full of tears he started his story.

"I and the gang was up at the barn one night last week. The others wanted to look at dirty pictures and they said I was too young so they sent me over to the other side of the wall. I was angry and I started to kick the straw around and I found this." He pulled out of his pocket a flat, shiny blue narrow box.

"What is it?" asked Smith, although he already knew what the box was.

"It's a dart box," Andrew said.

"Go on tell them the rest," urged his dad.

"It's Bobby's box. I seed him with it, when I waited outside the pub for me dad. So I knew it was 'is. See it has B for Bobby scratched on it."

"Which pub was that Mr. Brice?"

"The Black Swan just off Elm Grove. I'd seen the William's boy in there often."

"When did you find this Andrew?"

"Last Monday night when we were up there, regular like."

"Why did you keep it for so long? You knew by then that Bobby was dead. Why keep it?"

"'cause I didn't think it was important, I was scared, besides he doesn't need 'em now and he was a really good player. I just wanted them."

"I am going to keep this now, I'll give you a receipt and then you can go home." Jones carefully placed the box in a brown envelope. The box had a shiny, flat surface and he was hopeful that forensics could lift some fingerprints from its surface. Bobby's or just possibly his killer's.

Returning to the Knowles family Jones asked Tom to tell him exactly when his group had been up to the barn during the past month.

"We go up every Monday after tea and then sometimes on a Wednesday"

"What time do you go and for how long?" asked Smith.

"Usually after tea about six-thirty and stay until about nine o'clock."

"Wait" said Maggie. "The Monday before last we didn't go at all. Mum you were sick, puking all over the place and I had to stay home to look after you."

"That's right the other kids came looking for you and they all went back home after chatting with our Maggie and Tom. They were here about an hour. I could hear their noise from my bedroom." said Mrs. Knowles

"But all of us did go up last Monday," said Tom.

"What did you do up there. Anything in particular?" Smith asked. Tom looked sheepishly at his mother and then to the floor.

"We looked at dirty pictures, but we sent the youngest into the next bit. We don't want no bother with their dads."

Maggie went across to her mother and tucked her arm into her mother's.

"We don't mean to cause you trouble mum, but there's nothing much to do in Whitehawk and we get bored at home." Mrs. Knowles was silent. Tom just sat there looking down at his feet.

"What am I to do with them, my old man ran off and I don't have much money. Tom is a good boy really but he's bored too."

"Just make sure that we never have need to get them down here again," said Jones.

Mrs. Knowles had stopped crying and stood up ready to take her kids home. She turned to the officers, "That's so easy for you to say. You try bringing up kids on your own without any money and with hardly any jobs about." And with that she stalked out of his office.

Smith chuckled as he gathered up his notes. "Didn't take her long to get her fighting spirit back."

Before Jones packed up for the night he played a hunch and made a long telephone call to his friend Adam Fletcher in London.

Next morning Jones found several memos on his blotter. One was from Masters, who had helped the mechanic strip down the black van; he wanted to see Smith or Jones as soon as possible. A second one was a telephone message from forensics concerning the dart box, the third was from Smith letting Jones know that he had the report from their visit to Rottingdean ready and the typed report of the interviews with the Knowles and Brice families. The last memo, but by no means the least, was a curtly written message from Supt. Young wanting Jones's presence in his office at eleven o'clock that morning to go over the William's case. Quickly Jones went across to Smith's office where his Sgt was going through his memos.

"I have to meet with Supt. Young at eleven this morning so I need you to do this follow up with the garage, have those interviews ready as well as statements from Mr. Plant and Mrs. Adams and bring me anything else you have. I have a message to call forensics, hope we get some results there." Returning to his desk Jones began to prepare his comments for the Supt.

Knocking on the door, at precisely eleven o'clock, Jones felt well prepared to meet his senior officer. But to his surprise both the Chief Constable of the Sussex Constabulary and the Chief Inspector of Detectives were seated at the desk with Young. Jones was relieved that he had worn his better suit that day. As he took his place at one end of the square table Supt. Young began the introductions explaining that the senior officer's presence was in response to the general public's concern that Brighton was becoming a refuge for London's gangsters.

Young continued, "Each of us," waving his arm to signify all those present, "have received calls from local Members of Parliament, local magistrates and from our more affluent citizens who are looking for answers as to why we haven't solved the murder of the Williams boy. These officers are here to receive confirmation that the C.I.D. is doing it's very best to solve this situation and that they can report back that some progress is being made." Sitting down the Supt. asked his Inspector "What have you got so far?"

Jones put his notes on the table, stood up and started his report by giving statistical information regarding the number of people interviewed, the variety of places visited and the forensic work presently being done.

"Yes but what else do you have?" Jones did not take Young's impatience as a criticism as he knew that the Super was very unhappy at having his own superior officer at this meeting so he quickly began again.

"Sir, we have uncovered several items of interest during the course of our investigation into Bobby Williams' murder. We have established that Bobby was seen getting into a small black van outside the Black Swan on that Monday evening. A witness has stated that there were two men in the car. One of average height the other was a very large man. We have established that Bobby Williams was recently in the old barn up on the Racehill. We have also been able to ascertain that that was where he was attacked. The blood on a chunk of wood found in that barn has been identified as matching the blood of the victim. We have also recovered a box of darts, from the same barn, with the initial "B' carved on it which has been identified as belonging to the victim. I am waiting for forensics to see if there are any prints on the box. We have interviewed each of the members of a gang that frequent that old barn but so far we are unable to make a connection to the murder." Jones continued. "We have a witness who states that a small black van was parked illegally outside her house that Monday morning, was gone during the day but was back there Tuesday morning. This happened on a road close to Preston Park Station. Our witness called in to the station to report it abandoned a few days later and we picked it up. The vehicle is presently undergoing a forensic search in our garage. We also have a witness who saw a black van leaving the building site late that same Monday evening. We have also located the car that Williams is said to have driven."

"Do you think one of the young people committed the murder?" asked the C.C.

"At first we thought we were onto something but I cannot connect them with the van or see how they could possibly have moved the body from the barn down to the Baker Street site." The Chief Constable kept tapping his pen on the table, finally he spoke again.

"Why did you go out to interview Mr. Moore?" before Jones could explain the Chief said, "I know Mr. Moore personally and he called me over the weekend. He was very angry that you had visited him for what he felt was no apparent reason. Moore also said that you were rude and aggressive towards him. Well I want an explanation Jones!" The C.C. was almost shouting while pointing his pen at Jones.

Jones stood up and apologized for any misunderstanding that had arisen but denied that he or his men had been rude or aggressive. But he was pleased that he had caused Moore some anxious moments. He really did not like that man. He then went on to explain the mystery of a robbery that had apparently taken place, at a house with a description fitting that of Mr. Moore's house, yet not one person in the village had reported any such event, and as Bobby Williams had told his friend that he did do the job then Jones felt it necessary to go to the house to see for himself.

"Do you actually suspect Moore of being involved in his murder?" the C.C barked across the table, "the very idea is preposterous."

Jones quickly replied "No sir, at least not just yet. I am suspicious that he was robbed yet didn't report that to the police. Things like that always puzzle me."

The meeting finally came to a close with the Supt. offering Jones more men as needed and getting Jones' assurance that the murder was number one priority. Jones hurried back to his office calling to Smith as he put his overcoat on.

"Let's get out." Smith quickly appeared at his side wondering what the rush was. "Oh I just need to get away before the Brass comes around the corner and asks questions about the killers that I can't answer." Smith nodded, and they hurriedly left the building.

They decided to go for a beer and a sandwich at the pub just behind Hannington's. It was always busy during the summer months but now that most tourists had gone it was a good place for a quiet break.

"I needed that" said Jones after downing half of his beer. Silently they tucked into their sandwiches. Smith knew that his boss was not in a conversational mood and needed a quiet time just to get over the morning's meeting. It was not until they had both finished that Jones talked about the case.

"We have a murdered boy and no concrete connection with any of the information so far. I no longer believe that the Knowles boy was involved in the killing but the barn could be the killing spot. I don't like Moore, yet I have nothing on him, just a nasty feeling. I feel that we have reached a dead end. People are being helpful but obviously they know little." He sighed. "Why don't you go back to the office, meet up with young Masters and get all the loose ends sorted out, follow up on that memo from forensics, and any paper work that needs to be completed. I need to get away from my desk, get some air and try to develop in my mind a new line of investigation. I am going to take a walk through the streets between North Road and Trafalgar Street and then back here to these antique shops."

"Are you looking for anything in particular?" asked Smith.

"Yes and no, I like the small junk shops. I like to rummage around in those and the antique ones, just to see what they have. But I am going to be looking for any shops that specialize in snuffboxes. Moore had quite a collection of them and I'm curious why some are in London being appraised. So I'm just going to have a look."

"Do you want company?" asked Smith.

"No thanks, I will just pretend that I am a tourist looking for a bargain!" Smith was quite happy to have some time to spend on his paperwork and he could keep an eye on those young constables. Jones paid for the lunch and the two men parted, going in opposite directions.

CHAPTER EIGHTEEN

Moore was anxiously waiting for his two enforcers to report back on what information they had got from Miller. He was an impatient man and paced up and down on the expensive carpet as he waited. They had both returned immediately from Sussex and were now on their way to his flat. At last the porter called to say they were coming up.

"Now I will find out who organized the robbery and finish him off." The flat bell rang and he let them in.

"Well" demanded Moore.

"Miller knew that there was somebody else giving orders to the leader, someone who the leader was going to meet in London the day after to hand over the goods and to get paid. Miller swore he didn't know the leader's name but admitted that he had worked with him before on a couple of jobs on the south coast. The so-called Leader had a reputation of being a 'fixer'. None of the thieves knew whose house it was that they were robbing and Miller's job was just to cut the alarm, open the safe and relock it after the package was taken. Then get out with the others. Miller said he didn't know the kid," said the one enforcer, finishing up his report.

"Well," said Moore, "We need to find the third burglar who should be able to lead us to whoever is behind the robbery. So neither the kid nor Miller had any idea who this person was?"

"No," was their answer.

Moore knew that he could easily contact these two when he was closer to learning the identity of the third man. Now he needed to get rid of them Moore didn't like these two hanging around his flat. Giving each a packet of money he hustled them out of the apartment and down the service lift to the back entrance. As they left Moore instructed them to be available for his next call while warning them against doing anything that could possibly jeopardize this business.

Moore was very angry as he climbed back up the stairs. Two of the thieves were dead yet he still had few clues about who ordered the burglary and why. The kid had said he thought that the third man was from the south as he went up to London but came back that evening to pay him and Miller. Miller had said that the third man was known as 'the fixer' and worked exclusively in the south. Moore intended to return home that evening and from there he planned to call one of his informers to put the word out on the street that there was a large amount of money being offered in return for any information on a man known as the 'fixer'.

Moore's associate would follow up on any information given and contact Moore only when he had a definite name and location. Moore was convinced that once he had this third burglar in his power then the name of the person behind the operation would soon be his. Then he would get his jewels back and he would be secure again.

Moore smiled to himself as he remembered his other reason for returning that evening. He was hosting a dinner party in aid of the local dramatic society and his guest list included several notable people. It always gave Moore tremendous satisfaction that as a citizen of note in Rottingdean, guests, such as the Chief Constable of Sussex and his wife were flattered to be invited. He had dined with the Chief Constable several times and as he listened to the pompous opinionating of the man Moore silently thought of how this man would react if he ever found out Moore's true business.

Moore had also invited his solicitor Saville-Smythe, for he really liked this man, Moore felt that he was honest and particularly well informed on current business and commercial trends, which was helpful to a man in Moore's line of business. Although after the events of the last few days Moore had been wondering whether when he was finished dealing with the rest of the thieves, he should buy property far away from Sussex, perhaps in North Wales. Once he had his package back he had enough assets to ensure his children's futures and to retire on. Moore was going to put the proposal to his solicitor after the dinner party.

The dinner party was a great success with everyone committing themselves to a financial pledge to assist the dramatic society. But it was the conversation that always intrigued Moore. As usual the Chief Constable was the guest who had the most to say, expounding his theories on why the crime rate had risen so drastically in the past two years. He blamed it mostly on the lack of moral fibre of modern youth and the laxity of parents in coping with their rebellious children. Discipline and hard work was the C.C's answer to youth crime.

"Send them all to Borstal. That'll teach them."

The only reason that Moore invited such a man to his house was to protect his own position in both the local community and the larger Sussex community and of course to enjoy the total irony of the situation. Moore had manipulated the C.C. into admonishing his Inspector for visiting Moore on such a vague item as a suspected burglary. But on the other hand Moore knew that Jones was no fool and Moore had to ensure that all the time he and the C.C. were social friends Jones would have to keep his distance.

Moore turned to his solicitor, unlike the others around the dinner table Saville-Smythe was totally aware of Moore's duplicity.

"Saville-Smythe you must have an opinion about the youth of today after all you are the one among us who deals with some of these cases in the courts."

"I abhor the growing propensity for violence that is gradually taking hold of our society at all age levels. I don't think that the youngsters of today are really bad. If families are having difficulty making ends meet then it's only natural that the children will feel the effects of that worry. I think we should be more tolerant of family situations and be thankful that we are not a society who believes in the ultimate value of the gun."

The Reverend Davies was surprising liberal in his views stating his belief that there was good in all people, even the youngsters.

"It's my belief," The grey haired man stated, "that attendance at church should be mandatory and that only then would people return to the old values of decency and honesty."

The Reverend's wife did offer a view but that was interrupted by dessert.

CHAPTER NINETEEN

It was Tuesday late morning before Jones received anything new on the Williams' case. Local forensics had sent the print from the dart box up to the Yard in case they could identify the print as there was nothing locally. There was nothing on the van or Bobby's car. Just as he was gathering up his notes to leave the 'phone rang.

"Jones here," he said, he was silent for a moment and then said, "Okay we'll be right over". He called over to Smith.

"Dr Marshall has a body over at his place that he wants us to take a look at. Similar injuries to Bobby." Smith hurried to get his coat and order a car, no walking this time.

Pushing the double doors open they found Dr Marshall just inside waiting for them. Without delay he went ahead with his findings.

"Gentlemen, this afternoon we are looking at a male, between the ages of fourty and forty-five, about five feet ten inches tall and weighing approximately thirteen stone. No identification at all on the body which was found yesterday lying beside the down-rail just north of Clayton Tunnel. It was brought here, as per procedures. At first I thought that it was just an accident victim so I didn't get to it until this afternoon. Especially as superficially the victim's injuries seemed consistent with a fall from a moving train. However after registering those injuries I was still left with a series of blows that were more consistent with a sustained, brutal beating." Dr Marshall paused for a moment to consult his notes.

"I take it you feel that these injuries are similar to the Williams' boy?" asked Jones.

"Most definitely" stated Marshall as he moved closer to the body. "Here, here and here are marks left by a knuckleduster and these two bruises have been left by a swinging chain. Also several of the internal organs are exhibiting signs of stress which again is similar to the earlier victim."

"Would you say that it was highly probable that both victims were beaten by the same person or persons?' queried Jones, looking at the body on the stretcher.

"Yes most certainly. I took photos of the chain marks and the bruises on the boy's body and look see for yourself. The length of the marks left by chain links are the same size and the bruises are in roughly the same position on both victims," said Marshall. "The injuries have a pattern about them as if the beating has stages which grow increasingly more brutal until death occurred."

"Let me get this straight," said Jones. "This man was badly beaten and then thrown from the train, most probably the London to Brighton side."

"Was he dead when he was thrown out?" asked Smith.

"That is more difficult to determine," said Marshall "but if he wasn't dead then he was certainly dying."

"Are you sure that he came from the train and not simply thrown down the embankment?"

"Yes," echoed the pathologist "his legs were broken in so many places that it had to be as a result of hitting the wall of the tunnel at speed. To my knowledge there is no decent road access to the railway tunnel itself, so unless he was carried across the fields he either fell out or was pushed out of the train."

"Can you estimate when he died?" asked Jones.

"My best estimate would be Saturday night or possibly Sunday morning. Most probably Saturday night."

Smith suggested that this time fingerprints be taken of the dead man just in case he had a record. Jones also suggested that Dr Marshall have all the victim's personal belongings sent over to his office. The officers thanked Marshall and left the mortuary both pondering this new development.

"This could be a vital piece in the mystery of Bobby's death. This one could possibly be a member of the gang who did the robbery, obviously an older much tougher man although I noticed his hands were quite soft and well cared for. I want you to set up a meeting with the railway police and the couple who first reported the body. Let's suggest about 3 o'clock this afternoon at their house.

The house where the group met was quite extraordinary. It was built as an integral part of the structure directly above the north entrance of the railway tunnel. Even the design itself was extraordinary as it was in the shape of a gothic arch with castellated turrets on either side. The house was in fact a small cottage perched directly above the north entrance.

On the journey from Brighton Smith had explained that in 1861 the tunnel was the site of a triple train accident. Those were the days of hand signalling and three trains from Brighton, the 8.28, the 8.30 and the 8.35, were mistakenly allowed to enter the tunnel almost at once. Tragically they caught each other up in the mile long tunnel and twenty-three passengers were killed.

"It was after that accident that mechanical signals were first introduced," explained Smith

The laneway to the house was quite crowded with two bicycles and one car already parked and their owners standing around awaiting the detectives. Introductions were made and then they all trooped into the little cottage to see exactly where the body had been sighted. Mr. and Mrs. Fellows occupied the cottage. Mr. Fellows was a railway signalman working out of the signal box just past Burgess Hill station. Smith asked Mrs. Fellows to explain exactly what had happened yesterday morning. Just as Mrs. Fellowes was about to speak the entire house began to shake and a tremendous roar went through the rooms. Jones looked at Smith.

"That'll be the three minutes past ten out of Brighton," Fellows said, smiling at the Inspector's face, "be another one along soon."

"I suppose you get used to the noise, doesn't it ever bother you?" Jones asked

"Oh yes especially in the summer at the weekends when they put on extra trains for the day trippers. That's when I go to my sisters," she explained.

"Mrs. Fellowes shall we get back to the events yesterday?"
Nervously twisting the bottom of her apron Mrs. Fellows said she had spotted the body as she was standing at her kitchen window making her breakfast cup of tea.

"We get up early in the mornings as Mr. Fellows has to be at work by seven o'clock on this shift. We were a little at sixes and sevens as we spent Saturda4y and Sunday at my sisters over at Horsham and I had a load of washing to do, I was in here just having a quiet cup of tea, it was getting light and I knew I had to get started soon. So I got up and went over to the sink to wash my cup when I spotted this bundle in the bramble bushes. At first I thought it was some old clothing that had blown around but as I looked I could make out two shoes. I left it a while and started the boiler for my wash but then I took a second look, it was still there. I didn't go down to see. I turned off the boiler, put on my coat and cycled over to Mr. Brown's. He has a car and a telephone. So he rang the Burgess Hill station, 'because that's where the railway police have their office. Then he went to pick up Constable Harris and bring him here. I cycled back here and waited for them." Mrs. Fellows finished, quite out of breath.

"Mr. Brown told me what Mrs. Fellows had told him about the shoes," said P.C. Harris. "I walked to the edge of the embankment to see but then I waited for George here, 'cause it looked like the bundle was on the line."

"Then what happened?" asked Jones turning to the railway police officer.

"Constable Harris and I scrambled down the bank. It's very steep there and covered with heavy bramble bushes, as you can see. The thing was just beside the tunnel entrance on the down side. Once we were halfway down the embankment we could see it was a body. It was under some bushes, very close to the line." He looked at Jones, "It was lying real awkward like, as if everything was broken. We came back up and I cycled back to my office and called the local medical examiner, Dr Blatchington, and an ambulance. They took about half an hour to get here. Then me, Dr Blatchington and P.C. Harris all went down again. We all looked at the body, mapped out where it was, noted the actual time and what trains had passed since dark last night."

"And then?"

"Well the doc said to move the body. Oh, that was a struggle I'll tell you, trying to get it up the embankment. One of the ambulance men tore his jacket trying to clear a path through those brambles. Anyway I marked where the body was found," said George pointing down to the red flag placed at the side of the lines. "The body was taken off to the Brighton mortuary, as my orders, and I went back to my office to finish my report. P.C. Harris here went back with Mrs. Fellows to make sure she was alright. I must admit the body did look smashed up a bit but what do you expect when it falls out of a moving train?" George concluded.

Jones hastened to assure them all that they had acted correctly and that the fact that it was more that an accident was found out by the expert examination of the pathologist.

"But," he said, "I would like a copy of all the notes that you have made as they will help us in our investigations." Anxious to return to Brighton to see if this new event was related to their investigations the two detectives hastily drank their piping hot tea and left.

"Well sir, what do you think we have here?" asked Smith as soon as they were on the main road. Jones was looking out of the car window just tapping his forefinger on the ledge, just tapping and thinking. Smith waited, he was used to the Inspector's silences Then Jones spoke.

"At present we have several different events that don't seem to be connected," he mused. "I mean, is this body really connected to the Williams case or is it just coincidence? Is this another member of the gang who did Rottingdean or was it just some drunk coming down from a night on the town in London who happened to open the door on the wrong side of the train to get out and fell into the tunnel wall ? Was it a Londoner coming into Brighton or a Brighton man coming home? We really need to have an identity before jumping to any conclusions." Smith listened, nodding in agreement.

"Perhaps will get that tomorrow," he said as he concentrated on the tricky driving around Preston Circus. "By the way how did you get on with your walk yesterday, any joy there?" he asked.

"There are certainly some interesting people living and doing business in that area from Trafalgar Street to North Street. I pretended to be just an ordinary shopper but several of the shopkeepers were suspicious of me and were very pleased when I left their shop. One or two even put up the shutters and closed their shop just as I reached their door and it certainly wasn't closing time. Turning to Smith he smiled and said, "You know I think I will do that more often!"

"Yes," agreed Smith, "that would be good because I seem to have worn out my welcome with those beggars." They both smiled at the thought.

"What about you, did Masters find anything in the car, anything at all?"

"Yes, he did. Oh dear, I am sorry this second body threw it out of my head. Masters brought me a small collar tab with the letters S.R. embroidered in red. It was found tucked down in the metal parts of the gearshift box beside the driver's seat. The tab had been identified as similar to those worn by Southern Railway Permanent Way staff, those who worked on the trains or on the stations. This was yesterday when I got back from lunch. I sent out constables to find information especially from the railway staff who either worked at Preston Park or who started or ended their workdays there. I told them to concentrate on the Monday of Bobby's death. Those reports should be in by now sir. I'll check as soon as we get back."

Jones didn't hold out much hope as it really was such a small piece of cloth.

Smith was going over each constable's written report on the Williams case summarizing salient facts and looking for connections when Jones walked by.

"Sir, do you remember our visit to Mrs. Adams of Clermont Terrace near Preston Park station?" Smith called out.

"Yes, about the van."

"Well we have two different members of the platform staff at Preston Park who have reported something odd to our men. The first man said that when he was collecting tickets from the nine-twelve semi-fast from London he noticed this railway man go through the barrier showing a very dirty and bent railway pass. Apparently he told him that he had better get a new one as if it was an Inspector on duty he wouldn't let him through. Also he, the ticket collector, could never remember having a worker go through at that time before. He intended to ask the man where he had been but the man disappeared very quickly."

"And the second?" asked Jones.

"This was a different ticket collector, but on the same day, he was on duty for the last semi-fast to London and he let a worker through the barrier. He thought it was a bit late so apparently he said something to the man who mumbled back something about doing the milk run and the ticket collector didn't really think much about it until later when he realized that workers for the milk run usually left on the eight-ten."

"If the man dressed as a railway worker was the one who picked up the black van from outside Mrs. Adams and returned it later that night perhaps, just perhaps, we have a connection here with Bobby." Jones was exited. "Perhaps he went up to the Black Swan with a partner, picked up Bobby, killed him in the barn and dumped his body on the way back to catch the train."

"That would fit all the times for the sightings of the van. But why would somebody go to such lengths to kill a young man. What on earth was Bobby involved in?"

Just then the telephone rang, "Sorry to bother you sir but there's a Mrs. Watts and her daughter sitting here by the front desk. They want to speak to you and said they are not leaving until they do."

"Okay I'll be down." Calling to Smith he strode down the corridor.

"Hello Mrs. Watts, Pamela what's the problem?"

"It's Pamela, she is so upset since Bobby died. I thought it was just sadness but now I think that Pam is hiding something and she doesn't know what to do about it. She won't eat or go out. She doesn't even want to come shopping with me. I asked her why and she said that she didn't want anybody to see her. Honestly Mr. Jones I think she's frightened." Mrs. Watts was holding her daughter's hand, and looking at Pam said "But I persuaded her to come and see you. After all she should be safe in a police station."

"Let's go along to my office and see if we can sort this out. Will you get some tea Sgt?" Settling the mother and daughter in chairs Jones said to Pamela.

"I could get a policewoman to sit in if you wish?" Pamela shook her head. "Pamela your mother is very concerned about you. We are all very sorry about what happened to Bobby. We are moving along in the investigation but we need all the help we can get. Perhaps you know something that would help us. Perhaps whatever is frightening you is the key to the whole mystery of why Bobby was killed?"

Pamela mumbled something through her handkerchief and just as she was lifting her head to speak Smith arrived with four mugs of tea.

The young girl wiped at her tears and then started to rummage in her handbag. Jones thought she was looking for a clean hanky but that was not it. Instead Pamela pulled out two smallish packages, each wrapped in tissue paper. She removed the tissue paper very carefully and laid the objects lovingly on the desk. For a moment there was absolute silence in the room. Jones picked the objects up, he knew what they were and he had a good idea where they had come from. But he waited for Pam to speak.

"My Bobby gave these to me a couple of days after he did that job. He said that they were for our future and that I was to look after them for him."

"Do you know what they are Pamela?"

"Yes, antique snuffboxes. Bobby told me he took four of them from the house and nobody knew he'd done it."

"Where are the others?"

"He sold them to a dealer to get money for his weekend in London."

"Did Bobby tell you anything more about his the job?"

"No, well only that he was the getaway driver and the others went upstairs for other stuff."

"How many others were there, did he say?"

"No, just others" said Pam. "I'm frightened. I don't want to get killed like Bobby did."

Mrs. Watts tried to comfort her sobbing daughter and Smith quietly left the room to order a car to take the two back home. Again Jones thanked Mrs. Watts for bringing Pamela in and then he spoke directly to Pamela thanking her for coming in to see him and that he felt the snuffboxes would be extremely helpful in tracking down Bobby's killer.

"Well, well, well" said Jones as Smith returned, "this is a stroke of luck. When I was out on my walk yesterday I paid particular attention to those places that specialized in small bits of antiques," said Jones, "I found three that sell small pieces of Georgian or Victorian silver, such as snuffboxes, pepper pots, miniature sewing boxes. You know the kind of thing I mean. I would like to go back to those shops officially, with Bobby's photo and see what that brings in."

Smith looked at his notebook, "Why don't we do it about ten o'clock tomorrow? I have sent Masters out to re-interview those workers at Preston Park station and it could be a couple of days before London gets back to us on the fingerprints for the Clayton Tunnel victim."

Taking the snuffboxes out of his desk drawer along with his office magnifying glass, Jones slowly turned them over in his hand. They were magnificent. The first one was a Huntsman and Hounds silver table snuffbox; about 3 three inches long with carvings of huntsman and foxes in the lid. It had the name Fribourg and Treyer of London on the underside. The second one was far more ornate. It was circular in shape, about four inches diameter, it was made of painted tortoiseshell and showed a lady seated, playing a harp. Jones was sure that this one would fetch at least a thousand pounds while the other would fetch about two hundred. Both of these were quality items so why had their theft not been reported. Of course Jones could list many reasons why owners did not call the police when their valuables were stolen and he was anticipating an interesting interview when finally the owner of the snuffboxes was identified. But that event was probably a few days away yet.

But Jones knew that four snuffboxes and an unreported robbery by Bobby and mates was too much of a coincidence. He was feeling much more confident that the investigation was moving in the right direction and he couldn't help but feel just a little smug about his suspicions of Mr. Moore and determined that he would bring as much pressure as possible on the man to get to the bottom of Bobby's murder.

Just as Jones was leaving his office Supt. Young came around the corner.

"Ah just the man I wanted to see. Let's go in shall we?" and led the way back into Jones" office. Smith had seen the approach of Young and had wisely ducked back into his own office.

"I want to know how you are getting on with the William's case. The C.C, has been on my back again complaining that you are not moving quickly enough."

Quickly explaining about the second alleged murder victim, the information given by the ticket collectors at Preston Park station and the discovery of more information about the original robbery, Jones was able to satisfy Young that the investigation had speeded up and he had a better idea of who he was looking for now.

"Forensic was able to lift a print from the dart box but we couldn't match it down here. Dr Marshall said that it looked very similar to the print he found on the belt of the body found near Clayton Tunnel. Also, Marshall sent the tunnel victim's prints to London, as being an older man he just might have a record from up there. But even if he didn't have a criminal record there might be something on him at War Records. So now I'm waiting for those results to come through."

Jones had also sent the second victim's clothes over to forensic to see if it was possible to lift a fingerprint of his assailant from any of the belongings. The Inspector knew that chances of getting prints off of material were very difficult, but it was worth a try.

"Actually sir, I asked Inspector MacDonald at the Yard for assistance on this matter. I believe you know that we are working together on the smuggling business."

"Well all right, just let me know when you know more. I certainly hope you are not considering the C.C's friend Mr Moore

"Yes, Mr. Moore that's right" answered Jones purposefully ignoring the first part of the Super's question. The Super then asked how the smuggling investigation was going and if Jones had been up to the Yard to offer his ideas?

"That investigation is not moving very quickly. We had absolutely no results at all on those two incidents last week. I am going up later this week to see Macdonald."

"Just make sure you keep me informed," said the Super.

"Of course sir," said Jones to his super's retreating back glad to be free before he felt obliged to talk about young Pamela's revelation.

CHAPTER TWENTY

"Ready now," said Jones. "Do you have the photographs?"

"Right here," answered Smith pointing to his jacket pocket, "I'll just pick up my coat. Are we walking or riding?"

"Oh, walk I think," said Jones "save the Super some petrol money" he smiled at Smith as he said it knowing that Smith still ran a family Austin and was always concerned about the price of petrol.

The first shop that they entered was owned by an older woman who apparently, had bought the shop long before the War. She was dressed in long black clothing with snowy, white hair piled on top of her head fixed by a large Spanish looking comb. She wore wire rimmed glass and a gold watch on a long, gold chain hung about her neck. She came out from behind the counter to greet her customers.

"Good afternoon gentlemen, how can I help you?"

Jones and Smith both showed her their warrants cards and explained that they were trying to track down some stolen snuffboxes. Immediately she drew herself up to her full height and indignantly stated.

"I am an honest dealer in antiques. I don't deal in rubbish or in anything that is in any way questionable. So I don't know that I can be of any assistance." She abruptly turned back to her counter and began rearranging some necklaces.

"We didn't mean any offence we would just like you to look at this photograph and let us know if you have ever seen this young man," Smith said, showing her Bobby's photo. Turning, she took the photo.

"No. I have never seen this lad." and then in a much gentler tone added "oh dear. This is the dead boy from the building site isn't it?"

"Yes it is. We are trying to trace his movements for the few days before he died. We have reason to believe he was trying to sell two antique snuffboxes." Smith showed her the photographs of the snuffboxes.

Scrutinizing the photos she replied, "These are valuable, especially the round tortoiseshell one. But I have never handled these, sorry."

The woman apologized for her curtness and suggested that they try the two shops further in The Lanes.

The second shop was on the corner of Ship Street beside the large antiquarian bookshop. Smith pushed open the door and was assailed by a cloud of cigarette smoke. Instinctively coughing Smith entered the shop and held the door for Jones who was already grimacing at the stale smell that escaped as the door was opened. The owner was sitting at a desk seemingly busy with his paperwork. He turned to look them over and only then did he slowly lower himself from his chair. He was a small, bent, wizened man wearing thick glasses and with a cigarette behind his ear. His suit was black and was probably, in its day, expensive but now it was shiny with age and the front of the jacket bore the stains of many years of falling cigarette ash.

"Yes can I help you?" he asked, as the officers moved towards the counter. Showing their warrant cards Jones asked him if he sold many snuffboxes.

"Yes they are very popular just now," he answered and proceeded to pull a tray out from under his counter.

Smith moved forward, "Have you ever seen these two articles before?" he asked, as he pushed the photo' of the two snuffboxes into the man's vision. The owner quickly pushed his tray of jewellery and bits back in under the counter knowing there would be no sales today with these two.

"No, I have never handled anything as expensive as that round one. Never seen them before," and handed the photo back.

Jones then thrust Bobby's photo forward "Has this young man ever been in trying to sell you snuffboxes?" The proprietor looked at the photo for several minutes. He had seen Bobby even before that day Bobby had come into his shop. "Yes I have. One day he came in, looked around and then asked about the price of a snuffbox. I chased him out 'cause I thought he was just checking out my place for one of those robberies." He took the half-smoked cigarette from behind his ear and lit it, slowly taking a couple of puffs before asking Jones "What's this all about then?"

"Don't you recognize this young man?"

"Yes I told you he came into my shop"

"This is the young man whose body was found on the Baker street site a week or so ago."

"Oh my gawd, I had no idea," he staggered and almost collapsed against his counter, making some of his jewellery jingle. But he knew that he had nothing to do with what had happened to Bobby, he didn't even know his name. He was being entirely truthful and was ready to help. Mopping his face with a mangy looking handkerchief he stated.

"Actually the lad went across to Brian's café over there and then I think I saw him going down into Meetinghouse Lane. That's all I know." They thanked him for his help and quickly left the shop drawing in fresh air as soon as they were outside.

"Let's try that café and see if they can tell us more. Besides I could do with a cup of tea," said Jones, already striding across the pavement.

They took a table at the rear and waited to be served.

"We'd like a couple of teas and two scones," said Smith "but we also want to talk to the owner, Brian I believe his name is, about Bobby Williams." showing the café owner his warrant card.

"I am Brian but I don't know any Bobby Williams," he told them. Smith quickly pulled out Bobby's photo and showed Brian.

"That's the boy who was murdered isn't it? I knew him as Jack. I always called him Jack when he came in for tea. I didn't know that wasn't his real name." Brian told them about the afternoon that Bobby (Jack) came in and asked to borrow a mac' and a tie. "He bought them back after half an hour and then he left. He was whistling as he went. He must have made a good deal somewhere. Poor little bugger."

Leaving the café they walked through the narrow, cobbled street to the third and last shop of interest to them. A young girl was at the counter and she called out a brightly.

"Good afternoon, can I help you?"

Showing their cards again Jones said, "We do hope so. Is the owner in?"

"No," said Sheila "Mr. Sinclair has just gone across to the bank he won't be long, can I help you?" Smith drew out Bobby's photo

"Have you ever seen this young man before?" he said, placing it on the counter. Sheila immediately became upset.

"That's the boy that was killed isn't it?"

"Yes, do you know him?" asked Jones.

"I didn't know his name but he came in here selling two snuffboxes. He would only deal with Mr. Sinclair but I heard them negotiating a price. Mr. Sinclair gave him some money and the young man left. That's all I know, honest."

By now Sheila was in tears, she had known since reading about Bobby's death that she was accidentally involved in something really nasty but she was too frightened to go to the police herself and possibly get Mr. Sinclair into trouble and possibly lose her job. Jones asked to see the boxes but Sheila was adamant that they were no longer in the shop. She hadn't seen them from that day. Jones asked if she would have any idea who the boxes might have belonged to previously and Sheila went to a back drawer and pulled out a large accounts book.

"It might be in here," she said, "Mr. Sinclair puts all his sales in this book. But I don't know when he sold them the first time." Jones sat at the desk and started looking through the book. Once he recognized Sinclair's method of coding different items, he moved much more quickly through the pages. Sinclair had sold five snuffboxes in the past two years, each one to the same buyer.

"Look at this Smith," Jones pointed to the name- Mr. Moore of Rottingdean.

Sheila had recovered by now but was concerned that she was in trouble. As Jones was reassuring her a man entered the shop.

"Oh look here is Mr. Sinclair. Thank goodness. Mr. Sinclair these men are police officers." As Smith went through the process of explaining why they were in his shop the owner's face went from pink to white to grey. He grabbed the counter for support and then sat down heavily on his chair. Smith offered him Bobby's photograph.

"Your assistant has been telling us that this young man came into your shop trying to sell two snuffboxes." Sandy nodded and Smith continued, "We have also learned that about two years ago those two snuffboxes had been sold to a Mr. Moore who lives in Rottingdean. Is that correct?" By now Sinclair was mopping his face with a white handkerchief.

"Yes, yes," he muttered.

Sheila was weeping and called out "I didn't mean to get you in trouble Mr. Sinclair." Smith went across to her,

"Mr. Sinclair isn't in any trouble, yet. It was legal to buy those boxes from Bobby as long as he didn't know that they were stolen."

Jones was standing close to Sinclair and suddenly pushed the photos of Pamela's snuffboxes into his face. Sinclair almost collapsed.

"Do you recognize these?' asked Jones.

"Yes I sold those about two years ago."

"To whom?" Jones spoke very sternly, leaning down to the bent over man.

"Mr. Moore," whispered Sinclair.

"Who did you say, I can't hear you?"

"Mr. Moore, out at Rottingdean," Sinclair almost collapsed.

Jones paced up and down; he knew that the entire success of the investigation depended on Sinclair's answer to his next question. He moved back across the shop until he was almost touching Sinclair's shoulder.

"Mr. Sinclair I am going to ask you a question that you must answer truthfully. Do you understand?" Sinclair's forehead was speckled with droplets of sweat that ran down the sides of his face onto his shirt collar. He had given up mopping his face and now sat pale and trembling waiting for Jones' question.

"Mr. Sinclair did you contact Mr. Moore regarding the two snuffboxes that this young man bought in to sell?"

"God help me. Yes I did call Mr. Moore."

"What was Moore's response to your call?"

"He said that he reckoned some young window cleaner had snuck into the house and pinched them."

"Did he seem concerned?"

"Not at all, he just wanted them back, so I sent them out by messenger"

"So Moore has the two that you bought from this young man in the photograph?"

"Yes, yes oh God yes. What have I done?" was Sinclair's tortured reply.

"Is there anything else you would like to add?" Jones asked. Sinclair, a broken man, looked up at Jones shaking his head,

“I didn’t mean the boy any harm. Why would he be killed over a few snuffboxes?”

“That is what we mean to find out. I’ll expect you down at the station tomorrow with those accounts books.” With a great effort Sinclair nodded. Smith explained to Sheila that an officer would visit her the next morning to have her sign her statement and record anything else that she might have remembered.

“Would nine-thirty be convenient?” he asked.

“Yes I’ll be here then.” Sheila said, as she closed the door behind them.

Jones was so excited he was almost skipping across the cobblestones.

“Yes,” he said to Smith, “we both knew that there was something rotten about Mr. ‘high and mighty’ flaming Moore.

The next day Jones had planned that he and Smith would go over every piece of information they had so far. He had a large piece of paper spread out on his desk on which he had drawn three circles.

“These represent the areas that are involved in this case. This centre one is Rottingdean where everything started with the robbery. This second one is Brighton where we found Bobby’s body, the black van and the stolen snuffboxes. The third circle is London. That is where I think the killers came from, and the second body was on the down line so that could be another link to London.” Jones stood up studying his plan.

The telephone rang, “Jones here. Hello Mac, do you have something for me?” Jones grabbed a pad and began writing very quickly.

“Thanks a lot Mac. I owe you one. Any luck with the print that we got from the dart box. No. Okay. Although we have no concrete evidence we do believe that both the boy and Miller were killed by the same men and they are Londoners.” Jones listened “Thanks again.” and replaced the receiver.

“Listen to this Jack our second body is that of Ted ‘Dusty’ Miller, a well-known safe cracker. A man who had been employed by Special Services but is retired now. He lived in Sutton, Surrey and there were rumours that he had connections to several London gangs. He had never been convicted but his prints were held at the Home Office due to his work in operations in Europe."

Jones went back to his diagram adding Miller's name in as a London- connection. He looked at his paper and then sat back slowly tapping his pencil against his teeth.

"Sgt I want you to take Masters and go and visit Rottingdean again. This time I want you to speak only the housekeeper. I want you to see if she can identify the snuffboxes that Pamela gave us, as the two that are supposed to be in London for evaluation. Be sure that Moore is not home when you go."

"I will. Young Masters is just writing up his report from his visit to Sinclair's antique shop. He shouldn't be long now. I'll call Mrs. Stevens to see whether Moore is in London or at home. If he's away we could go out there this afternoon." Jones agreed but added that he would like to hear Masters verbal report about his visit when they returned. That's if they were able to go today. Half an hour later Smith popped his head around Jones' door,

"We are on our way. See you in about an hour. Oh Mr. Sackville-Smythe is here to see you Inspector. Shall I send him up?"

"No I'll be down, ask him to wait .I'll just be a couple of minutes."

"Good morning have you made any more progress on our missing man?" Jones asked the solicitor, as he entered the room.

"Yes and its becoming more bizarre by the day. I followed through with the bank that he had given as his reference and found that they had a name and address in Spain as well as here. They do have copies of all of his documents for his cars and his yacht. But they knew very little about the man himself|"

"Any previous history?"

"They knew he had arrived from South Africa about five years ago when he deposited a huge amount of money in their bank, he told them he had sold a cement business over there. Apparently he guarded his privacy well, never telling anyone at the bank about his personal life. As far as the bank was concerned there was no wife or children and he hadn't made a will. I have a former school chum who has a business in Johannesburg and I asked him to make discreet enquiries about our Mr.

Forest but nobody was familiar with our man's name or the business that he said he sold"

"And the board of Directors at the track have no idea where he came from, what he does or where he got his money?" asked Jones

"No I did ask the bank manager if he could tell me how our man spent his money but all he would say is that he travelled back to Africa once a year and to Amsterdam at least twice very year. What does that mean Inspector?"

Jones was very thoughtful and then spoke. "It would seem to me that having a good sized yacht, often travelling the English Channel and having connections in both South Africa and Amsterdam and having a pile of money and very little known about his background, it is very tempting to surmise that he could be smuggling, probably diamonds."

"I had wondered that myself." replied the solicitor as he closed his file.

"What next?" he asked

"Leave it with me for a few days I will contact my opposite number at the Yard and let him know what you have found and see what his reaction is."

"What about the missing money, was that ever found?"

"Actually I sent out an officer from fraud and he discovered that the office manager was systematically stealing by creating false invoices. But a trap was set and she fell in. The Board wanted to keep it very quiet so they dismissed her and she has already left the area." Just as the solicitor was leaving Jones casually asked "Do you know Mr. Moore very well?"

"Oh yes. He has been a client for several years now and I often do land deals for him. He buys property on speculation hoping to make a profit."

"Is he very successful?"

"Yes he is as he is well liked locally. I was out at his house for a dinner last week. The guests included some county officials, very enjoyable although my friend does enjoy putting people on the spot with his questions. Actually your CC was there too. I'm not too sure he enjoyed it thought!" the solicitor said with a wry smile'

"Well, at least he was fed, our CC always enjoys a good meal thanks again, good day."

The results of the visit to Rottingdean were very positive. Smith and Masters had met Mrs. Stevens just as she was bringing in the washing from the line. Masters had carried the washing basket into the kitchen for her and then Smith asked her if she could describe the two snuffboxes that were still in London.

"She was puzzled by our request but invited us to go into the lounge where she said she could better describe those that were missing. Mrs. Stevens said that one had some kind of dog on the lid and the other one was round with a lady playing a harp. I showed her the photos and pretended that I had taken them from an antique catalogue. Mrs. Stevens agreed that the ones in the photo were very similar to Mr. Moore's snuffboxes."

"Excellent," smiled Jones "we are getting closer."

"Sir," interrupted Masters, "while the Sgt was talking to Mrs. Stevens I took a little walk around the property and behind the house at the end of a muddy lane there was a shed that had car tracks going up to the door. I couldn't get in as it had a large padlock but it looked as though it had been used recently."

"Good work Masters, make sure you include that in your notes." said Jones "Now constable what about your morning trip?"

"Sir, the assistant Sheila was there as we expected, but no sign of Mr. Sinclair. I took down all the information that the Sgt told me to ask about and then I asked her if she would like to go out for lunch. She did hesitate at first and then said, "Well Mr. Sinclair left me in charge so I can shut the shop if I want." which she did and we went to the small café around the corner.

"This is a summary of the new information that Sheila gave me." Masters then began to read from his notebook. "Sinclair had asked her if she knew Bobby and she had told him that often she had seen Bobby at the Elm Grove bus stop over on North Street. She also said that after Bobby left the shop that afternoon Sinclair made a very short, private phone call and then suddenly left the shop and was gone for over an hour. She thinks he went up to the pub, 'most unusual at that time of day' was Sheila's comment." Masters continued, "According to Sheila,

Sinclair received a long distance call about five o'clock and then he left for the day. The following Monday afternoon she had an appointment with her dentist and Mr. Sinclair said she could go straight home afterwards as he was expecting an important customer down from London and he would close the shop to regular customers. Sheila also said that Sinclair had been very agitated about something since the Inspector was in; she thought it must have been about the phone call he told you about yesterday. Sinclair did not come in today. He called and told Sheila that his aunt was ill again and that he was going down to Southampton for a few days to look after her." Again Masters consulted his notes "Sinclair also told Sheila, not to talk about the snuffboxes to anybody except the police and that she had to put the day's takings into the bank and pay herself on Friday. And that's about all," said the young constable closing his notebook.

"How did she seem to you?" asked Smith.

"Well Sgt she had recognized Bobby's photo in the paper and was very upset and felt that somehow she was responsible especially after telling Sinclair about seeing Bobby at the bus stop. She seems to have been worrying herself sick whether to call the police or not. I tried to assure her that she wasn't in trouble but she still started to cry."

"Might you see her again?" asked Jones thoughtfully.

"Yes I rather liked her."

"Well it would seem that our antique dealer is on the run. We'll give him a couple of days. Masters you keep in touch with Sheila to check if he calls her. In fact call her now and see if she has any information on Sinclair's aunt. Perhaps we can trace Sinclair through the aunt. He was a very scared man and, I imagine, easily intimidated by Moore and now frightened by what he had set in motion with his phone call. Perhaps rather than wait for him to return we should ask the Hampshire constabulary to watch out for him and keep him safe, as he will be a material witness when this case comes to the courts. Could you look after that Smith?" Jones thanked both Smith and Masters for a job well done. After Smith closed the door behind him Jones leant back in his chair and stretched. He was feeling satisfied with the events of the day he really felt that the investigation was finally getting somewhere.

Before leaving he placed a call to London. Adam answered but had very little information to give Jones. "I went around to that Gentleman's Club that you said but the secretary had only the Rottingdean contact information for Moore and said that he had no idea of Moore's business affairs. Sorry I don't have anything for you. Oh Dai," he continued. "I have been keeping my ears open around the docks and all and there does seem to be something going on. There seems to be some anger about dockers not being paid properly for 'extra work'. Not sure what that means but will keep listening."

"Thanks Adam I will get back to you. Family okay? Good to hear you. Bye."

CHAPTER TWENTY ONE

Early the next morning Mrs. Stevens was very surprised to find the two police officers waiting on the doorstep as she answered the knock.

"I believe Mr. Moore is in, could we see him please?" and with that Jones took a step across the threshold leaving the housekeeper no option but to step back.

"My goodness yes Mr. Moore is in but he is working in his office. Is he expecting you?" asked the flustered woman.

"No, but we need to see him now. Please tell him we are here." Mrs. Stevens hurried down the corridor while the officers followed behind, close enough that Moore would see them when Mrs. Stevens opened the door.

"What now?" was the explosive response from inside the room?

"Good morning Mr. Moore we came early to catch you before you left for London," said a very polite Inspector Jones.

"I am very busy I have a train to catch and I'm already running late.

"Oh we thought you always drove up to the City." Moore looked daggers at Smith before looking down at his desk and fiddling with some papers.

"Well mostly I do but not today. But what is this visit all about?"

"Well sir we are looking for an antique dealer by the name of Sinclair, Sandy Sinclair, I believe is his name. Yesterday we were questioning him about some stolen antiques and today he didn't turn up to his shop. We know that you have had dealings with him in the past so we wondered if you might know where he is?" Moore walked across to the window away from Jones.

"Yes I do know Sinclair, but I haven't done business with him for a year or so." He turned back to the officers, "Did you know he had an elderly aunt down Southampton way perhaps he is there."

"Thank you we will follow that up. So glad we caught you in this morning."

"Yes, well you could have telephoned."

"Ah yes but you see Mr. Moore we are still investigating these robberies including an alleged one here. If I remember correctly it was you Mr. Moore who was so critical of our efforts to solve these crimes so we are here, following up, doing our job. We were wondering if any of those three could be connected, in any way, to the local rumours of a robbery supposedly done here and we are wondering if they are connected, in any way."

"Oh very well but I know nothing about one here in the village. Is that all then as I have to go?"

"Oh yes, thank you again. Oh I was talking with your solicitor yesterday. He has been very helpful in tracing the background of a missing man. Yes very helpful," finished Jones who joined a smiling Smith down the front path.

"You certainly gave him a fright this morning. Did you see his face before he suddenly went over to the window? And his hands were shaking as he was moving the papers around."

"There is something very unpleasant about that man, something evil and I mean to learn what he has been up to," said Jones. "Although we have no proof Mr. Moore is top of my list of suspects and I'm wondering what his next step will be."

As soon as the men had left, Moore called his friend the Chief Constable.

"You told me that you had Jones under control but that dammed Inspector has just left. He was on my doorstep almost before breakfast. This is not good enough. I am a respectable citizen with a legitimate business and I will not stand for this harassment." He shouted down the telephone.

"Yes, yes, you must calm down Alex. I will call Supt. Young immediately and put a stop to Jones. Goodbye." The C.C. put the telephone down hastily not being willing to bandy words with the irate Moore.

Jones was not the least surprised to have Supt. Young waiting in his office for him. Young opened his mouth to speak but before he could get a word out Jones started.

"I know he has called you and yes we did go out there with nothing but a gut feeling of the man's involvement. I wanted to shake him up and hopefully his response will create a few connections for us. Sorry I didn't warn you but I didn't want you to say that I couldn't go."

"You can guess that my conversation with the C.C. wasn't at all pleasant, but, I suppose if it helps to catch a murderer I can take it."

Jones visit angered Moore, not because Jones had anything on Moore but simply because Moore felt he was above annoying things like police 'fishing expeditions' and he returned to London more determined to get hold of information on those involved in the robbery. It was in the afternoon that something turned up. According to Moore's associate the informant had not been working the streets very long and consequently the first contact with him was not given much importance. It was only when the snitch claimed to know the name of The Fixer and his present whereabouts, did Moore's associate take notice.

The meeting was scheduled to take place in the Buffet at Brighton Station. A place that was always busy both with train passengers just waiting out time and local workers who came in from the surrounding area knowing that they could have a good plain meal at reasonable rates. The buffet stood sideways to the station concourse and with all its windows, a customer could see the Arrivals and Departure Board, the platform gates and the majority of passengers entering or leaving the station.

"It's about that kid that was killed. I was sitting right 'ere at this very table having my tea when I looked up and saw the kid waiting at the Smiff's stall. 'Course I didn't know who "e was then but later I recognized 'im. I didn't know the man that the kid met up with but I did see the man give the kid a package, a package small enough to shove in his pocket."

"Who was the man?"

"Well I didn't know him then but by chance I met him again in a pub down Blatchington Road. Apparently he had just moved into a new flat around there."

"What else? Have you any idea where he is now?"

The informant was silent. Suddenly he was very frightened of the well -dressed man sitting opposite him. He sensed an evil about this man; he recognized in the steely eyes a ruthlessness that would tolerate no mistakes. Suddenly he began to shake as he suddenly realized what his greed had got him into. They had not asked his name but Jim knew that if he backed out now somebody would be sent to find him as surely as they were now looking for Napier. These people who needed Napier were no softies, they had already killed the boy and were probably going to kill Napier. He breathed in; at least he didn't know why they wanted Napier. But now he had to decide whether to give up Napier and enjoy the large amount of money offered or back out, stay poor and be looking over his shoulder every day. Finally, with a deep sigh he made his decision.

"His name is Napier, Thomas Napier and I have a telephone number of the café nearby where he is staying, somewhere down in the West Country," he said.

"Well that's a start, now we have to get Napier up here so that he can be questioned."

"I'll be going then." said Jim grabbing his cap from the table and quickly moving across to the door.

"Not so fast." A large man, who had been sitting across from them, moved in to block his escape.

"Ere, what going on then?"

"The money will be yours. I have it here in my pocket, when you have telephoned the café and told Napier to come back to Hove."

"'ey I can't do that, that's not part of the deal it was only information that was wanted not 'elp to catch him."

Jim blustered as he continued to struggle against the arms of the large man. There were other people in the Buffet but as usual everybody was busy with their own business, soothing a crying baby, reading the paper, arguing loudly with a spouse, or just sitting quietly deaf to all around.

"No Napier, no money. That was the deal and as I hold the money. Perhaps you would like to think again," suggested the well-dressed man.

Jim sat down heavily knowing that he had no chance against these men. He would do whatever they wanted and they wanted him as the bait to draw Napier back to Sussex.

"What do you want me to say then?"

"Does he live in digs?'

"Yes."

"Landlady?"

"Yes."

"Then tell him that there has been a fire and his landlady says that he must come back to get his stuff, what's left of it, before the house is pulled down."

"When shall I do it?"

"What's wrong with now, the café should be open. There's a 'phone box out there. Fred will go with you. Here's some silver for the call." A smaller man sitting in the far corner left his table and moved across to the men.

"What another one. Blimey how many do you 'ave 'ere?"

The two men left the Buffet and crossed to the telephone box that sat at the corner of the ticket office, well in view of the men watching from the Buffet. Jim lifted up the receiver, gave the operator the number and then put the required money into the slot and waited ready to press button A. The traditional burr, burr seemed very loud in his ear.

"'arbour café here." The coins went down

"Can I speak to Mr. Napier?"

"Sorry mate he's just gone 'ome."

"Can I leave him an urgent message then?"

"Yes okay. Gimmee a minute, Oh where's me pencil. Okay go ahead"

"Please tell Napier that this is a message from his landlady, that there's been a fire and he'd better get back to collect all his clothes and things before they pull the house down. He'd better be quick about it."

"I'll send my boy up to the house with this. Who is calling?"

"Oh I live in one of the other rooms. The landlady was hurt in the fire and she asked me to call. He'll know who I am. Thanks mate."

With that phone went back to its cradle. The two men went back across to the railway Buffet but now they needed Napier's Hove address. Jim swore he didn't know it but after more threats of bodily harm the traitorous friend confessed to following Napier home one night. Jim was well paid for his betrayal.

Napier had settled in with his sister down in Looe. He was able to pick up some casual work on the fishing boats and could pay towards his food expenses. Gradually he began to feel more secure. He had always enjoyed being on the water and he knew that he was safe when he was out on the fishing boat miles from shore. But walking to and fro the harbour was the time he was most anxious, he still had no real evidence that he was being followed, just a feeling of danger so he kept a close eye on who was around him. In a small place like Looe, especially this late in the season most of the tourists had left so it was easy to pick out strangers like him.

When the fishing boats returned about noon Napier always went over to the local newsagents to buy a London newspaper. Then he would move across to the little café, have his lunch while scanning the pages for anything to do with the robbery. He saw the article headed '*Mysterious death on the Southern Railway*' but just glanced down the lines not paying much heed until near the bottom. '*Body identified as that of Ted 'Dusty' Miller of Croydon'*. His heart stopped beating, he read on, paying no attention to his cooling chips. Napier began to feel dizzy, he was shivering but he was also hot all over, he could hardly maintain his balance on his chair and had to hold on to the table to stay upright .

"Oh my God they got Dusty!" he cried out. He was alone in the café as the other fisherman had finished their meals and left. Napier began to panic. "The bastards. What did they want to kill Dusty for he didn't know anything?" Then self-preservation kicked in.

"Oh my God what am I going to do they must be looking for me now?"

He spoke aloud, but nobody was there to hear him. There was a brief moment of relief as he had remembered that he hadn't told Dusty that he had moved from Brighton into Hove and his name wasn't in the telephone directory and young Bobby had no idea who he was. Gathering up the paper under his arm Napier climbed the hill to his cousin's place. He stumbled as he walked knowing that he had never been so frightened for his own life.

"What should I do? Where can I go? What options do I have?"

He knew he had to get away as far as possible from London and the South Coast. Perhaps Scotland or even chance the ferry to Ireland, or should he go to the police and tell them about the Rottingdean job. Napier knew he couldn't stay where he was. Once inside the small house Napier went immediately to his bedroom knowing it was decision time and that his life could very well depend on his next move.

Suddenly there was loud banging on the front door. His clothes fell from his nerveless fingers "Oh my God they're here already." Cautiously pulling back his curtains he saw with great relief that it was just young Willy from the café. "Be down," yelled Napier.

Willy was sitting on the doorstep still out of breathe from running up the hill.

"Me dad sent this up for you," said the young boy waving a scrap of paper in Napier's face. "Me dad said it was urgent. Summat about a fire."

And the boy took off back down the hill. Napier tore open the note to read the few words explaining the café owner had received a telephone call from a friend of Napier's, a man, telling him that Napier's lodgings in Hove had caught fire and that the landlady wanted him to return to sort out his belongings before the building was pulled down. The note added that the caller said he was a fellow lodger. Napier's first reaction was to worry about the items he had left in his rooms in Hove and he started to plan a trip back.

Suddenly he stood up remembering that all the other lodgers in his house were in fact women. Four young girls who had started work at the DuBarry factory near Hove station. He stumbled to a chair. Who had known he was here? He was sure that his landlady would not be involved in anything that would cause him harm and he had left behind some items that he wanted to keep. But why the pretence about being a fellow lodger and why the urgency to get back to Hove? What had happened? Who else had he told of his plans? Jim? But why would Jim betray him, he was a friend. Napier was at a loss to answer these questions but regardless he now knew that he had to move on. Whoever was looking for him now had the name of his local café and surely they would soon be down in Looe.

Now he focused on where he should go. He certainly couldn't go back east, it had to be north to Scotland or west into Wales. Wales was the closest and had the better train service so that was it. Surely he could hide out in the mountains of South Wales until he felt safe to return to Sussex.

"But when would that be?" wondered Napier, "When I don't even know who's after me."

Having determined his course of action Napier felt more confident about his future. Quickly packing his few belongings he wrote a note to his cousin explaining that he had been called back to Hove and left the note as evidence. Then he walked down the hill to the station avoiding any conversation with passing villagers and bought a ticket for Hove, changing trains at Southampton.

His plan was to get off at Southampton and then buy another ticket back down to the West coast and then gradually make his way by some of the less travelled routes into Newport and then up the Valley. He knew that he would probably have to sleep rough for a while and planned to pick up food on the way. By going back east the ticket collector, who knew him, would confirm that Napier was going back to Hove as Southampton was the change station for Sussex.

Before leaving Southampton for Wales Napier had one more task to do. From a telephone box at Southampton station Napier asked the operator for Hove 52741. Napier let the bell ring twice then hung up. He got his money back and then repeated the process but then waited to see if anybody would answer at the other end.

"Yes" said a deep voice.

"Leader here, Williams and Miller both worked on my Rottingdean team. Both have been murdered. I am getting out!"

Napier slammed down the telephone, turned towards the trains and began his flight away from danger.

CHAPTER TWENTY TWO

The Boss was alarmed. The call from Napier had unnerved him. In his time he had financed many large heists along the south coast but not one of them had ended in a murder. Obviously he had badly underestimated Moore and the lengths he would go to retrieve his jewels. Why were these particular stones so important? But what to do now? Napier had gone into hiding. But what should he do to protect himself? He felt pretty confident that none of the murder victims had any idea who he was. And he was confident that Napier only knew of his own existence by the telephone number. He went carefully over the meeting in London and felt that he had covered his tracks very well, especially the change of disguise in the men's lavatories at Victoria.

Was this the end of his so-called career? Was this the end of the excitement and adrenalin fuelled risks that he so craved and so enjoyed? His daily job was worthwhile but held nothing compared to the passion and excitement that possessed him when he knew that criminals were out in the community working, stealing that is, for him. But everything had changed and now he knew he had to contrive a way to help bring Moore down. It preyed on his conscience that it was his own greed that had bought death to two men. He shuddered as he remembered reading about the discovery of each body but had paid little attention to the articles as he knew of no connection between himself and the victims. *Stealing jewels and other articles well that was fair game but murder. No that was too much he thought.*

Now he had to do something to stop the third man being found and killed. He could make an anonymous call to the police but that was tricky as they might trace his number. Perhaps an anonymous letter would be better. If he could get a total stranger to place a note through the letterbox at the police headquarters in Bartholomew Square, it would eventually get into the right hands. Better still, he thought to himself, don't involve another person, he could go around there in the very early morning, one or two o'clock and put it in himself. He would use a disguise, nobody takes much notice of a drunk at that time of the morning. The Boss began to feel more settled thinking that his actions could keep Napier safe. As he went upstairs to get ready for his late night trip into Brighton he decided to add a bonus to help the Inspector.

The Boss still had the pouch and its contents intact. In all his years dealing in rich client's estates he had never seen such glorious colour and such exquisitely cut stones. The jewels were the most valuable he had ever held in his hands. Since the robbery the Boss had been busily researching the provenance of each stone and discovered that the last recorded owner of each piece had declared their jewellery either stolen or lost. What the Boss really wanted to know was how someone like Moore got his hands on such fine pieces. Did he steal them? If so from whom, the owners or the insurance company, perhaps even from jewellers who had them for under-the-table resale. The small pieces were still in their original settings but the larger necklaces had been broken down into individual stones or settings, obviously ready for resale.

The Boss decided to send one of the brooches to Jones. He would include a clipping from an earlier catalogue that he kept for his research material. It was a catalogue of an internationally renowned auction House and actually contained a picture of this particular brooch when it was put up for sale before the war.

"That should be enough proof of its authenticity," he muttered to himself.

He hoped that his little offering to Jones would not only sew up Moore for the murders but the police would discover why Moore had these jewels in his possession.

Even with Scotland Yard's resources Mac was having difficulty finding information on the Miller incident but he assured Jones that he had sent two of his best detectives down to Surrey to make further enquires. But the Inspector was not a happy man, although pleased with what his team had found out so far he feared there would be another murder, the team leader. He was no closer to nailing Moore or anybody connected to the Rottingdean job. Although he had yet to find a connection with the three earlier jobs he had not ruled out the three men from London. As for what was actually stolen, it remained a mystery. The snuffboxes were, in fact, just a side issue as Jones was certain that young Williams had not been murdered over four snuffboxes but over the fact that he was part of the gang who stole something far more important from Moore's house.

That is the key item. Bobby wasn't killed because he stole the snuffboxes he was killed because he was there that night when something taken from the safe that started this killing spree. What was so vital to someone that they would organize such an elaborate theft and what was so vital to Moore that he would kill Bobby and possibly Miller too for stealing it?

Jones was staring at his location chart, all the known links were outlined but still a large question mark loomed over Moore's house. Jones knew all investigations have a tendency to plateau especially when new information dried up and clues lead only so far along the line of enquiry. But now he was hopeful that information about the unfortunate Miller would provide a new line of investigation.

The detective constable following Moore had reported to Jones that Moore had spent most of Thursday at his London club and then had taken a taxi to a block of flats in Mayfair. The doorman had shown the detective a list of the occupiers of the flats and then pointed out just three names whose lifestyle pattern fitted that of Moore but after hearing the physical description the doorman was sure that the man the detective was looking for was Mr. Mitchell.

"Mr. Mitchell always goes out to dinner at seven-thirty. So you could wait here until he leaves. Then you can see for yourself if he is your Mr. Moore" suggested the doorman. Promptly at seven-thirty both men heard the hum of the lift descending to the lobby. The detective sat himself across from the lift doors pretending to read a magazine.

"Good evening Mr. Mitchell," sang out the doorman as the well-dressed man stepped out of the lift.

"Ah yes John," was all the response he given as the man left the lobby.

"Is that your man?" the doorman asked after making sure the lobby was empty.

"Most definitely, your Mr. Mitchell is my Mr. Moore. Thanks for your help."

Listening to Mac's summary of the detective's report on Moore now known also as Mitchell, Jones decided to follow a hunch and ask his colleague to put both Moore and Mitchell into the London Record to see if anything came up. Mac added that that Moore stated his business as being that of Importer and Exporter a title which both detectives knew was a cover for all sorts of illegal activities.

It was time to pack up for the day hopefully tomorrow would bring fresh information and that he would perhaps see an end to this case quite soon. Jones had found the emotional stress quite exhausting so much was new to him. Dealing compassionately with grieve-stricken parents was difficult and time consuming but something that Jones knew he must do and do well. But dealing with those who have become involved, almost by accident, like Pamela, Bobby's girlfriend and Sheila the shop assistant and even young Bert, Bobby's best friend. Trying to reassure them that their lives were not in danger was something he had never been faced with. He had asked the beat policeman to keep an eye on all three, especially the girls and to let him know immediately when something, anything seemed not quite right.

But now, it was time for his walk home to Palmeria Square and just possibly a pint of the brown stuff at one of the pubs on Western Road. His flat was at the very top of a regency style house that Brighton and Hove were so famous for, and he loved it. He had four large high-ceilinged rooms but his furniture was sparse, even having one room that was still empty. The lounge was his favourite room, it was there that he kept his books and his precious record collection of Ella Fitzgerald's hits. Jones cooked for himself but chose to eat from a tray, sitting in his oversized armchair by the window looking out over the Channel, especially on those days when the gale force winds forced the rough sea to roll up the pebbled beach and spill over on to the esplanade. It was invigorating to watch and after he had finished supper he snatched up his raincoat, ran down the seven flights of stairs and walked out into the wind joining many other adventurous citizens who wanted to meet the challenge of the weather. Jones enjoyed the feeling of being turned and buffeted along the pavement, of hearing the roar of the waves and then the rattle as the receding water pulled the pebbles further down the beach. He trudged alongside the pebbly beach, until almost reaching the Palace Pier. He stopped then and walked to the end of the Banjo Groyne to stand for a few minutes catching the spray of the large waves as they crashed over the low wall and ran almost to his feet.

As he looked along the expanse of the beach he tried to imagine what it was like during the war. When miles upon miles of barbed wire had been dragged along the pebbles then hammered securely deep into the beach itself. When both piers were closed securely sealed off with wooden boards and more barbed wire Jack had described to him what it was like to walk along the esplanade and listen to the boom of the German guns over in France or to stand and watch for the flashes of explosions as the RAF dropped their bombs on the enemy territory. Jack had reminded Jones that the enemy coastline was barely 22 miles away.

"It was very difficult for people to really understand how close they were. All sorts of small boats would try to sneak in here no wonder we had barbed wire on our beaches and mines floating off the Piers."

Continuing along the beach he glanced at all the little kiosks and stalls set back under the esplanade. Some were still open trying to catch the late tourist trade and still offering ice cream, naughty postcards, cockles and whelks and all the other seaside junk that tourists love to collect. Turning he pulled ~~his~~ the collar of his raincoat up around his ears and headed back into the wind for home.

It was noon before Jones was able to get back to his office the next day, Plans for a new station were under discussion at the Town hall. Jones thought that he was too lowly a ranking officer for that kind of meeting but the Chief Detective Inspector had particularly asked Jones to go with him. Jones felt and said that this was really a waste of his time but the Chief saw it as an opportunity for his Inspector to keep in touch with the elected members of Brighton Town Council.

Smith knocked and came bursting into the office, so unlike Smith, was Jones's first thought.

"What's up?" he asked.

"Received a call from the Shoreham Harbour police reporting a badly beaten body had been discovered floating in the harbour yesterday afternoon. I don't know if it has any connection to the Williams' case or perhaps our missing yachtsman, but I felt we should take a look."

"Not another one!" exclaimed Jones. "Well let's get over there. It might have nothing to do with Bobby's case but perhaps it's a break in the smuggling that's going on. Perhaps this is our first link to continental side of operations. Oh and get Masters to call the mortuary and tell them to hang on to the body, I want to have a look at this one."

"I spoke with the Harbourmaster and he confirmed that that none of the boats presently berthed in the harbour were missing any hands, and no locals had been reported missing. He will call us if he hears anymore." Smith reported as they drove to the mortuary.

CHAPTER TWENTY THREE

After keeping a watch on the Hove flat for three days Moore believed that somehow Napier had sensed the danger in returning. Now Moore decided to send two of his men down to Looe to search out Napier and if he wasn't there to find out where he had gone to. Knowing that locals could be very reluctant to give information Moore chose two less conspicuous men. One was an ex-army officer from the ordinance corps who had been kicked out of the forces for stealing supplies, but Hemsley was a smart dresser with a quiet intelligent manner that had always helped him gain the confidence of others. Moore liked to use him when neat physical appearance and apparent sincerity was needed.

Hemsley and his colleague went down to Looe on separate trains and booked rooms in different B & Bs. Although neither of them had a photograph of Napier they had a reasonable physical description and they knew his favourite eating place. It was Hemsley who went into the café and explained to the proprietor that he had called a couple of days ago to speak to Napier about the fire at his flat.

"Yes I sent our Willy up to give him the note. Napier was there."

"What did he tell your son?"

"He just took the note and Willy came back."

"Would you kindly show me the house?"

"Yes, but you won't find anyone there. He went back to Hove and the young couple has gone to her parent's place in Somerset. I drove them to the station myself. Her and him and the baby. Gone for three weeks they are. Cancelled the milk and everything. You won't find anyone there."

Hemsley listened patiently to the café owner, politely thanked him for his help and left, knowing that later that evening, when it was dark he and his colleague would pay a visit to the house just in case Napier was still there. In the meantime he went to meet his colleague who was making enquiries at the railway station.

By the end of the day both men were satisfied that Napier was no longer in Looe. The ticket collector at the station had confirmed that a man answering Napier description had bought a ticket for Hove the evening of the phone call and that he saw him board the train. The men had also entered the small house and confirmed that it was empty.

Moore was not happy with this news. Usually his life revolved around his orders getting quick results, but the time it was taking to find Napier had him on edge. He knew that the longer Napier was free the chances of the police finding Moore's connection to the two killings grew greater with each passing hour. It was a race to get to Napier before Napier gave himself up to police. Moore was fearful that Napier might give himself up to the police before Moore could get to him, which would have disastrous consequences for himself as he would never get his jewels back then.

After the fruitless visit to Looe Moore sent his men back to Napier's flat in Hove with orders to pick up anything that could lead to Napier. In a duffle bag he had provided the men with bogus police officer's uniforms, two forged warrant cards and a forged search warrant. His orders were very simple: get in by means of the uniforms etc., pick up anything that relates to Napier such as postcards, photos etc. and get out without causing too much fuss. Travelling south by car very early the next morning Moore knew they could be in and out of the flat and back in London by evening.

Entering Moore's building by the service door and taking the service lift up to his floor they were in his flat without being seen. Half an hour later Moore's living room floor was covered in letters, bills and other assorted debris from Napier's flat.

"Well is this it?"

"Yes," said Hemsley, "he didn't have much in his flat, no framed photos, not much clothing, very little personal stuff but we bought all we could find."

"Any trouble getting in?"

"No the landlady was helpful and seemed genuinely concerned about her lodger."

"Well somehow we have to find Mr. bloody Napier and this mess doesn't look very helpful." Angrily he began to turn the papers over with his foot when he hit something heavier than just paper. A large paper envelope carefully sealed and tied with string.

"What's this then?" he asked as he tore at the envelope. "Look a photo album filled with old photos. This might be useful."

Moore began to leaf through the pages studying the fading family snaps looking for anything that could be a clue to Napier's whereabouts. Inside the front cover was a modern photo of a soldier on the back was written Aldershot 1946. Quickly he pulled out every snap that showed the same boy, turning them over to see what was written. Suddenly he yelled.

"We got you Napier," and he showed the others a photo of a young Napier taken at the seaside. On the back was written, 'taken at Rhyll, with Nana and Papa Napier.

"He's gone to Wales," said a triumphant Moore.

"I have something too," called out Hemsley. "Here's a photo with some soccer mates. Looks as though they are on holiday somewhere,' Taffy and Boyo at - Abergavenny' is written on the back."

"That's even better," chuckled Moore. "Now we have him."

It was very late but the front hall of the police station was still very busy. A fight had broken out in a billiard hall up by the Clock Tower and there were a number of rowdy people waiting to be booked by the desk Sgt During the melee a package was slipped unobserved onto the front desk. It was mid-morning when there was a soft knock on Jones' door, a W.P.C. stepped inside looking rather nervously at the Inspector.

"Yes what is it?" Jones asked.

"Sir, the desk Sgt asked me to bring this up to you. He's been very busy this morning and didn't notice this until a few minutes ago. He's very sorry sir," she gave Jones a small package and quickly closed his door as she left.

The package was small, no more than a couple of inches square. It was wrapped in white paper, which looked like a page from a school exercise book and then tied with white string. Jones turned it over several times. It just had JONES written on one side. Carefully he undid the string, unwrapped the paper and opened the box. Inside, in white tissue lay a magnificent emerald brooch and underneath the brooch was a very small, folded note. Tipping the brooch out of the box onto his blotter, Jones used his pen to gently remove the note.

On one side was hand printed **'DOZENS MOORE'** while on the other side was a snippet from a catalogue giving the past history of the jewel. Jones just stared at the two pieces and then striding across to the door shouted loudly for Smith. Half running along the corridor it was Smith's turn to say,

"What is it?"

"Sit down and look at what just dropped into my lap. Look at it and tell me what you think." Jones was smiling as he waited for Smith's comments.

"A very nervous person is pointing us and the jewellery towards Moore. Perhaps this is what was in the pouch. This and much more," speculated Smith. "Come on, I want to take this over to Hall's. The shop owner deals in precious stones and I want confirmation that we are not being had."

Jones signed a receipt for the brooch and they walked over to the office of Hall and Co, wholesalers in precious stones. Within half an hour the officers had returned to the station knowing that the brooch was genuine and the provenance printed on the note was accurate and at last they had, although anonymous, a concrete link to Moore.

Napier had spent the day at Abergavenny market helping his army buddy get the lambs ready for auction. He had spent the last week at Tom's place avoiding any strangers and just helping out generally. But Tom had had a good crop of lambs this past spring and now that they were fat enough to sell Tom needed Napier's help to get them over the mountains to market. It was late afternoon, the auction was over and the two friends were having a beer before heading back to the farm.

But the unsuspecting Napier ran into trouble, as he casually walked around the back to use the lavatory a blanket was thrown over his head and he was wrestled to the ground and hit twice on the head. Next thing he found himself on the floor of a car, face down, still wrapped in a blanket and with two large feet planted firmly on his back. He was only able to breathe by moving his head to the left, out of the carpet pile. He was terrified and without warning began to vomit into the blanket. A voice said,

"Can't have him suffocate before we get the information can we? Blindfold him then roll him over and gag him."

"No" mumbled Napier, "I'll be quiet." Napier knew instinctively that these were the same thugs who had probably killed Bobby and Dusty and that his life was about to come to a very painful end.

"Yea, you'll soon be very, very quiet," the driver called over his shoulder.

They drove for miles and as Napier listened to the occasional words of his captors he realized they were heading for London. It was very dark by the time the car slowed down and the men started to search for their destination.

"It was Warehouse number five," the driver said "Over there by those lights."

Slowly the car came to a halt and despite his struggles Napier was dragged out and dropped onto a wooden floor. Napier felt he was doomed, it was the end for him. He heard more footsteps and prayed that it was help but the two men who arrived were expected.

"Okay let's see what he knows," barked a new, more cultured voice. Napier was very conscious of a movement in close to his body. He drew himself in and steeled himself but it was no protection against the powerful kick that landed right in his belly. He screamed behind the gag but then another blow landed, and another and then a fourth. He tried to bring his legs up to protect his chest but each time somebody grabbed his legs and straightened him out for the coming blow. Finally it stopped. They sat him up and ripped off his gag then the new voice started to question him. Napier determined to stay quiet as long as he could, thinking that silence might prolong his life. Instead it only bought him more pain as his tormentors renewed their attack now using knuckledusters and a chain. Napier collapsed and was again dragged up to a sitting position. This time he started talking, but telling them only what Bobby or Mitchell would have known. He admitted to being the third burglar but had no idea who had ordered the job. His tormentors grew increasingly angry at Napier's stubbornness and a fury of blows landed on Napier's head. The man with the posh voice was screaming furiously as he realized finally, that Napier did not know the name of man behind the burglary. Napier was slipping in and out of consciousness when the questions suddenly changed focus.

"Did you ever see him? This so called Boss?" By this time Napier had slumped back down to the ground unable even to hold his head up. "Get him up. Shake him. Hold his head,"

"Now," the voice was in his ear. "Have you ever seen this so called Boss?"

"Yes," whispered Napier through his bloody, dislocated jaw.

"When?"

"In London when I gave him the leather pouch." Napier sagged at the knees.

"But I only saw the back of his hand," said Napier as he started to vomit again.

"Wait. Wait," he begged as he sank right to the ground "I saw a white scar on the back of his wrist."

"What kind of scar? "By then Napier had totally collapsed, lying perfectly still on the ground. He was semi-conscious and knew he was going to die, just like Bobby and Miller but he was determined not to give out the all-important telephone number. But the questioner was still not satisfied and ordered his thugs to keep beating him until he spoke again. But Napier never did.

"Well finish him off. Throw him down on the mud the tide will wash him away. Then clean up and go. I will telephone you soon."

Jones had been in contact with MacDonald at the Yard regarding the dead man found at Shoreham. He was frustrated. He knew that the longer the investigation went the possibility of a solution grew smaller. Why couldn't he make any headway with his enquiries? Superintendent Young was equally frustrated and needed a solution if only to get the C.C off his back, who was continually seeking assurance that his friend Moore, was not under suspicion. Young knew that Jones' instincts were usually right on the mark but found it really difficult to be patient.

The next morning Smith stopped Jones as he was going to his office.

"Good morning Sir I would like you to come with me to a flat on Blatchington Road."

"Why, what's the problem?'

"Well apparently Constable Hunter, a very reliable chap by all accounts, reported yesterday that he was speaking with the landlady of one of the lodging houses along Blatchington Road. The woman was annoyed at the mess the two policemen had left when they searched one of her flats last week. As you know we always let the man on the beat know when something is going down on their beat but Constable Hunter knew nothing of it and when he checked with his Sgt nobody knew a thing about this search."

"Are you telling me that this search was done by somebody masquerading as policemen?"

"According to the landlady both men were wearing police uniforms and showed her their warrant cards which she took to be genuine. She was concerned because her lodger, a Mr. Napier, had gone away very suddenly and she didn't know exactly where he was. Also the two men had only a small bag when they went into the flat but she watched as they left and then they were carrying two sacks full of stuff, paper she thought. I just called the substation and they do not know any more about the incident. The landlady did give them a description but it was so general it could have been anybody."

"Hmmm," said Jones "Keep the memo on your desk perhaps it is a lead but we can't see how it fits yet."

As Jones walked into his office the telephone was ringing.

"Yes Jones here."

"Adam here, how are Dai?"

"Well but really anxious to solve this boy's murder. I just cannot seem to get the pieces to fit together."

"Yes from all account it is a nasty one. But perhaps I might have come across something helpful for you. Last night I was checking things out near the docks when a man ran out of one of the loading bays yelling for help. He had found a body of a young man on the mud. The tide was coming in and the man needed help to drag the body up onto the dock. He thought the man was dead. But he wasn't. He certainly had been badly beaten but he was still breathing. Anyway I went in the ambulance with him and searched his clothing for any identity. I found two items:

a ticket stub from Looe to Hove with a change at Southampton and a telephone number Hove 52741. He was also muttering a word over and over, it sounded something like 'rotten'. He was very anxious to tell me and did manage to pull at my sleeve a couple of times"

"Where is he now Adam?"

"In Bart's Hospital, the doctor has put him in an induced coma for today to help heal his wounds. And before you ask I have cleared it with my Sgt for you to come and visit the victim."

"Excellent I will catch the afternoon train and meet you at the hospital by about four o'clock."

"Do you think it could be related to your case?"

"I don't know Adam but we do have a situation of a young man missing from Hove who was supposed to be in the West Country but whether he is involved in the robbery I don't know. It would seem two bogus policemen searched his flat so it has to be more than just a missing person. Anyway thanks. Look forward to seeing you later on." Jones went to put the receiver down and suddenly stopped.

"More than just a missing person! More, more, Moore!" he was shouting.

"You okay sir?" It was Smith at his door.

"Yes, yes, come on in. Adam Fletcher from the Met just called in reporting that a young man was pulled out of the Thames last night, barely alive. Adam thinks he is from Hove and he kept saying 'rotten' to Adam, in the ambulance. But I am wondering if he was actually saying "rotting as in Rottingdean."

"What on earth was he doing in the docks?" asked Smith.

"We don't know only that he had a ticket stub in his waistcoat pocket and it was Looe to Hove. Perhaps he is our missing man from Blatchington Road. Anyway I am going up to see him this afternoon Adam has already cleared it with his people. Oh, they also found a Hove telephone number, 52741. Could you look into that while I'm away?"

Jones asked if there was any news from forensics as they had taken Miller's belt, with its oversize brass buckle, in the hopes of lifting a print. They were hoping that one or other of them had grasped Miller's belt to hoist him out of the train window. But there was nothing as yet.

Inwardly Jones cursed, he felt that he was on the brink of solving the case but now he had to wait, again.

The telephone number found on the London man was certainly a local one but Smith found it was classified as an 'unlisted' number. Immediately he drove over to Telephone House, went to the third floor and asked to see the supervisor. Allan had previously provided Smith with information about numbers and subscribers but today Allan was up in the manager's office. Smith knew that no other person on that floor had the authority to give him the information he needed so he took a seat hoping that Allan would be back in soon. Smith wanted all the billing information about that telephone number and anything else that might be recorded on the application form.

At the London hospital the doctor allowed Jones to question his patient for just a few minutes as the victim was still not stable. Jones had devised questions that would hopefully give him the information they needed without taxing the patient too much. Conferring with the doctor outside the ward the officers learned that it was, in the doctor's opinion, a miracle that the man had survived all his injuries. He added that those who did this knew exactly where to hit to cause maximum damage.

The patient lay on his back with both legs encased in plaster and suspended from the ceiling. To the officers it looked as though every part of his body was bandaged the only flesh to be seen was his face and that was probably unrecognizable even to those who knew him. The Inspector drew a chair up close to the patient so that neither of them would have to shout. Fletcher remained by the door. Slowly Jones established the basic information; name, address, age, next of kin. Then he explained that he was from the Sussex police and was investigating the murder of Bobby Williams. Jones was surprised at the patient's response to Bobby's name, as the bed shook as Napier tried to lift his arms. The patient, now established as Thomas Napier, admitted that he wanted to tell the policemen about a burglary in Rottingdean.

"Go on," said Jones trying to stay calm. Haltingly Napier explained his involvement in the robbery, admitting that he had organized the job, had hired Williams and Miller and then had taken the pouch up to London. After letting Napier have a sip of water and a short rest Jones asked,

"Tell me about the London trip."

"I had to meet the Boss at Bishops Hotel. I gave him the pouch, I had not looked in it and then I travelled back to Brighton."

"What did this man look like?"

"I dunno. He was tall, wearing black and I never saw his face."

"Did you know the owner of the house in Rottingdean?'

"No."

"Any idea why the Boss wanted this job done?" Napier shook his head.

"What about the railway ticket stub?"

"When I saw in the paper about Bobby I didn't really think it was the robbery but I went down to my cousin's in Looe just in case." Napier closed his eyes. "Then when I read about Dusty Miller I knew I had to hide. I went to find my old army buddy and stayed on his farm in South Wales."

"How did they find you?"

"I don't know but they got me at Abergavenny market. They did speak about mates on the docks at Cardiff. They mugged me and then drove for hours. I didn't know I was in London until the doctor just told me."

Napier was able to give some descriptive details about the men who beat him, including that one had a cockney accent and the other was from the north, perhaps Birmingham. He also told Jones he was sure that he heard the name Fred used during the attack. He said there was a third man who he didn't see but who had a more cultured voice and seemed to be in charge.

"What did you tell them?"

"I told them the same that Bobby and Dusty must have said but I didn't tell the thugs how I was contacted for the job. They were going to kill me anyway so I told them about the scar on his wrist but I never told them about how I got my orders."

By now Napier was slipping in and out of consciousness and the doctor was hovering around the bed urging the detectives to leave. Napier began to speak very slowly.

"He would call me and let it ring three times he would do that several times. When I knew it was him I called that 52741 number, let it ring twice and hang up I'd do that once more. I'd wait then for about five minutes and he would call me back. Then it was about half an hour later that he called back with instructions. He used a public box, I could hear the button 'A' being pressed. If he wasn't there I would try again until we connected."

Napier was exhausted and the room was quiet except for the patient's heavy breathing. Then softly Jones asked,

"Tell me about the scar?"

"It was white and very thin I only saw it as his cuff slipped back when he gave me my pay." Napier head turned into the pillow and started to gasp for breath.

"That's enough for today," said the doctor firmly ushering the officers out of the ward.

"We will call his relatives to let them know his condition. Will you be coming again?"

"Somebody will," said Jones, "But hold off calling his relatives as it would be safer for your patient if his identity remains unknown for a few days. I want him moved to his own room and I am ordering a constable to watch him every hour of the day and night. Okay."

The doctor was quite taken aback by this request and hesitated for a while but Jones face presented him with no options so he hurried away to get the arrangements made. Jones arranged for Fletcher to take the first shift and then the local Sgt would make further assignments. He impressed on his colleague that the men on the door must never leave Napier's side as he had now become the major witness in the murders of Bobby and Miller.

CHAPTER TWENTY FOUR

Alex Moore sat at his desk wondering why, after he had spent so much money, he had so little information on who had organized the burglary at his home. He thought very little about the pain and sorrow his actions had caused, he viewed the beatings and even the subsequent deaths as being a means to an end. Moore could never survive knowing that there was a person out there who had bettered him. The jewellery was necessary to live but his pride was far more valuable to Moore and to restore his self-pride he must retrieve his property by whatever means were necessary.

The previous day Saville-Smythe had sent him the legal documents regarding the purchase of a property in Wales, with a note to say that the deal was moving along well and that he would be in his office in Hove should Moore wish to drop off the papers? Taking the documents out of the envelope Moore settled down to an afternoon's reading.

Quickly, reading through the first few pages that laid out the terms of the contract he reached forward for his fountain pen, as he did so he caught a glimpse of his own white wrist. Then it came to him. He remembered. He felt dizzy, momentarily thinking he was having a heart attack, his hand trembled as he placed the pen back down. Then came the rage.

"You bastard, all this time and it was you. You sodding bastard."

With shaking hands Moore unlocked the bottom draw of his desk and pulled out a revolver and a box of bullets. Shoving the loaded gun into his jacket pocket he raced down the stairs yelling to Mrs. Stevens,

"Gone to Brighton." Driving out of his laneway Moore fought to control his anger, well aware that if the police stopped him he would be arrested for carrying a loaded weapon.

Parking carelessly on Western Road Moore almost ran around the corner, took the steps two at a time and roughly pushed open the double glass door. Never even glancing at the receptionist he ran up the stairs straight across to Saville-Smythe's office and pushed open the door. Looking up in surprise the solicitor's face paled in fear as he saw who his visitor was and realized that his secret was out. He attempted to escape but Moore already had his gun trained on the solicitor's head.

"It was you all the time. Why did you do this to me? I thought we were friends," screamed Moore and squeezed the trigger.

The bullet missed Saville-Smythe and went into the wall just behind his head. Crouching down behind his desk Saville-Smythe wasn't so lucky this time and Moore's second bullet scraped across his cheek sending him to the floor. Moore, hearing the shouting and screaming from outside, again took aim at his friend on the floor.

"Serves you right. You betrayed me now, you are dead you bastard." Firing for the third time Moore flung open the door to the back entrance and fled, clattering his way down the iron back steps.

On arrival back in Brighton Jones was surprised to see Smith waiting at the barrier for him. Smith could hardly hold his news in,

"We have a name for that number sir and you will never guess in a thousand years whose it is." And gleefully gave Jones a small note.

"Look who it is!" Jones just stared at the name on the paper.

"My God, who would have guessed that, we had no information that led us to him? But wait, with the information that Napier gave to his attackers if they were working for Moore then Moore knows who did his house, for he would surely remember having seen a scar on his wrist."

Suddenly Jones was all haste,

"Quickly to the car. Get Masters to call Mrs. Stevens. Now. See where Moore is." Smith replaced the radio receiver.

"Masters said that Mrs. Stevens said Moore left for Brighton about twenty minutes ago. He was so angry he forgot to take his coat."

"Quickly," said Jones, "get a car for us and two backup squad cars to follow. Moore has made the connection and he will not hang around now he knows who the Boss is. We have to get there in time to prevent another killing."

Jones continued to shout instructions as they moved outside to their car.

"We must get to Brunswick Place quickly, that's where his office is. Use the sirens to clear the traffic away." Smith had called in destinations for the back-up drivers and the three cars would meet up at the bottom of West Street and continue along the seafront.

"The road is wider and there's less traffic." explained Smith who was sitting forward in his seat watching the traffic and occasionally checking behind to make sure the other cars were still with them. The noise of the sirens was deafening but other motorists did pull over and give them room to pass.

Within a few minutes they had sped west past the bottom of Preston Street, turned right at the corner of Brunswick Terrace, travelled up the north side of the Square until coming to a sudden stop at the curb of the Regency-style house close to the junction with Western Road. Jones sent Masters and some uniformed officers to cover the basement and back exits while he, Smith and two detective constables leapt up the concrete stairs, through the stained glass doors and into the main entrance. There were several sets of offices in the building but Jones knew that their quarry was on the first floor. Taking the stairs two at a time they barged into the reception office and ran full tilt into a crowd of very noisy people.

"What's going on?" yelled Jones at the top of his voice. The noise stopped very suddenly and he realized that the women were crying and holding each other.

"Find out," he said to Smith, he checked for the names on the inner door and went straight into the one he sought. Only one man was there, on the floor, holding his head. Jones bent over the man,

"Mr. Christopher Saville-Smythe, we meet again," smiled Jones. As the man nodded Smith yelled through the doorway,

"It sounds like Moore; they saw him leave down the back stairs. And he has a gun."

Jones yelled back, "Get downstairs and see what is happening I'll be down in a minute."

"Who shot you?" he asked the man on the floor.

"Moore" was the reply.

"Why?"

"Because he thinks that I arranged to have his house robbed."

"Did you?" demanded Jones.

"Yes." was the muffled reply.

Saville-Smythe was pale and continued to moan about his injury but Jones was not the least sympathetic. This man's greed had cost two lives and perhaps even a third, all for what? Jones turned to the waiting constable,

"Get this one looked after, it's just a flesh wound. Handcuff him. Get him taken to the station and book him, if he needs a doctor then get him one, but I want him held until we get there. He has a lot to answer for."

Outside in the reception area the employees who had heard the fight and the subsequent shots were huddled in a corner seeking mutual safety. Jones showed them his warrant card saying,

"We apologize for the interruption but we had reason to believe that Mr. Saville-Smythe's life was in danger. Fortunately he will live." Jones told the senior partner that he would be in contact as soon as they had Moore in custody. Then hurrying down the backstairs he found Smith kneeling over young Masters.

"The bastard shot him. And then he took off over that wall, I have two on foot chasing him and I have sent for reinforcements."

"How bad is he?" asked Jones, looking at the young constable on the ground.

"It's a shoulder wound sir, it looks as though it went in and out. Lots of blood but he will recover. He chased Moore sir. When he saw the gun he threw his truncheon at him and then tried to grab him. That's when he was shot."

They both heard the running steps of the ambulance men coming down the side path and waited as they put Masters on a stretcher ready to go to the hospital.

"Look after him," shouted Smith "he's quite the hero."

"Where is Moore now, anybody pick him up?"

"Yes sir, he was spotted two gardens down. He's running like a crazy man, waving his gun and pushing aside anything or anybody in his way."

"Anyone hurt?"

"Unfortunately a small boy was riding his bike up and down his garden path when Moore jumped his fence and simply knocked the kid over. Nothing more than a few bruises but the gun scared the kid. We have two uniforms on Moore's tail but they will not attempt to get him until he leaves the gardens. We don't want to force Moore into the homes and possibly take a hostage. A constable is going down the front of the houses to warn people to lock their doors, front and back, and not to come out until it's all over."

Once in the car Smith called all units to find out where each was. Then the radio came on.

"Sir, he is out of the garden area and is running down the pavement towards the seafront."

"Well he won't find much shelter along there; we'll probably catch him on the beach. He must hear the sirens and know that we are closing in," said Jones.

Another voice on the radio.

"Sir, the subject just knocked down an old lady who was on the crossing. He now appears to be heading towards the entrance to the West Pier. That won't do him any good he can't get onto the Pier it's closed. We have him now."

"Report in Sir" yelled Smith, "He's running down the centre of the main road waving his gun at the motorists. Our men are trying to get closer but he has fired the gun at them twice. Still running Sir"

"Get a car to seal off the road at the roundabout outside the Palace Pier. We'll try and contain him there and force him into that Pier," shouted Jones.

"Done Sir," yelled back Smith " Mobile Unit six is in place with Units four and five as back up."

"Cut him off and steer him onto the Pier then seal off the entrance. Evacuate everybody on the Pier and that includes all the fisherman at the end as soon as you can," ordered Jones.

Pulling up alongside two other squad cars Jones had already spotted four policemen moving towards the middle of the pier and sending any tourists back to the entrance. The thumping sound made by multiple pairs of boots running over the boards and the cries of alarm were the only noises to be heard. All traffic along the seafront had been halted and extra policemen had been bought in to keep the gathering crowd away from the action. Smith had a walkie-talkie now and was striding across to where a small command post was being set up. A voice came through

"Duncan here sir, I have an elderly couple who have been hurt, knocked down, I also have a young mother with a baby in the pram. I'm going to take them all into the pavilion and get them to lie down until it's over."

"Righto, we're coming through, we'll get them."

Smith then ordered more policemen onto the pier.

"Remember no heroics, Stay out of sight. He has a gun and will not be afraid to use it."

"Yes sarge." the response was almost swept away as four more sets of boots went thundering across the boards. Meanwhile Jones had moved onto the Pier and was walking swiftly to catch up with his men. He was very worried that Moore had a gun, concerned that he might have reloaded and would shoot it out with the police... His men were not armed and in the very rare case when the criminals had guns the policeman always had to be doubly careful to protect themselves and innocent bystanders. He heard Smith running up behind him.

"How many now Jack?'

"We have eight on the pier and two down on the beach, the tide is going out so they can get in a ways." Smith was interrupted by a high-pitched scream, two in fact, and the officers caught a glimpse of colour as something went over the side.

"Brown, Duncan-what's happening?"

"Brown here sir, he found two young girls hiding between the deckchairs up here. The bastard threw one over the rails and has the other hostage. Sir we need more assistance. Please hurry."

Both officers looked over the railings into the water. Smith spotted a head bobbing near the end of the Pier. Seconds later he saw a flash of dark blue enter the water.

"Brown here sir, Manning's got her. Just pulling her onto the pilings. Can you get somebody down there? The water is really cold."

"Yes" said Smith "where is Moore now?"

"He's almost at the end now I don't know where he thinks he can go from there. He's still got the other girl."

Smith and Jones moved up and joined the constables who were staying just yards behind Moore. They could hear the girl screaming to be released but Moore had his arm tightly around her waist, with his gun to her head.

Jones stepped forward and identified himself again to Moore.

"Put the gun down and let the girl go. You have nowhere to run. We know about your connection to Williams and Miller. It's all over now. Give up." But Moore was raving on about being double crossed, about being the victim rather than the criminal and fired his gun wildly in the air.

"Calm down," shouted Jones as he and Smith inched closer. "Just let the girl go and put the gun down. You are surrounded by police and by the sea there's nowhere to go."

"Oh yes there is," and pushing the girl down a small staircase Moore leapt over her and into the water just below the end of the Pier. They peered over the side and saw Moore surface and then start to swim out in the Channel. Suddenly Moore's head disappeared.

"Oh Christ the silly fool is going to drown himself," one of the constables shouted.

"Steady now," Smith spoke slowly to calm his men down. "Look he is back up and now he's waving at us. Do you think he wants us to help him? He had lost his gun."

"Well." said Jones wryly "He can stay there and tread water until we decide to get him."

Smith helped the girl back to her feet while reassuring her that her friend would soon be back on shore and she could wait for her in the police car. A small fishing boat was chugging its way out to get the girl and the policemen and Jones ordered a second boat out for Moore.

It took about an hour to get Moore into the boat and back to shore. He fought back as the men tried to pull him into the boat until one of them lost his patience and simply knocked Moore out, handcuffed him and sat on him in the bottom of the boat for the trip back to shore. Jones did not speak to Moore as he was hustled into the police car, but he did order that the prisoner be given dry clothes and detained until he and Smith were back in the station.

Smith checked that all his officers were accounted for, the elderly couple were on their way home by taxi, a policewoman escorted the young mother and her baby home and the two girls were taken home by police car. The lady, injured on the crossing had left in an ambulance and the command post had been dismantled. Smith rattled them off one by one to Jones and then finished up with

"All in a day's work, right sir."

"Yes Sgt but what a day it has been. We now have the Boss who wanted something special from Moore's safe. Something so important to Moore that he was prepared to stand by as two men were murdered and a third man beaten to within an inch of his life. So important that Moore carried a gun to use on his solicitor. It was as if Moore felt that he was above the law, he acted as though he was the victim and he handed out justice as he saw fit, vigilante style."

"Do we know what was in the pouch yet?" asked Smith.

"No. Hopefully that will all come out when we interview Saville-Smythe. I would like to interview him first and leave Moore until later. Perhaps by then MacDonald, from the Yard, will have further news on the two killers."

Back in his office Smith was quickly jotting down notes on the capture of Moore while Jones put the pieces of the case together and prepared his questions for Saville-Smythe. From the one robbery, that had probably taken three or four minutes to pull off, had evolved two murders with a third man close to death, a formerly respected solicitor with a bullet wound, an armed siege and the taking of two young hostages. Jones now knew that it was Saville-Smythe's greed that had set the terrible events in motion but what he really wanted to know was how long the solicitor had been leading a double life and what was so valuable to lead men to behave as Moore and Saville-Smythe had done.

CHAPTER TWENTY FIVE

The interview room was small with just one table and four wooden chairs. There was a small amount of light coming through the high window casting a glow on the traditional green and cream walls of government buildings. Everything purposely conspired to make the detainee feel less than comfortable.

Saville-Smythe was seated on one side of the table as Jones and Smith sat opposite with a uniformed officer standing against the wall behind the solicitor. Jones started by telling the solicitor that he was not being formally charged, as yet. That this meeting was simply to find out his involvement with Moore. Saville-Smythe insisted that he would not answer any questions until his own solicitor arrived. Just then a tap on the door announced the arrival of Mr. Hamilton who said that he would be acting on behalf of his colleague. Sgt Smith read out the caution and confirmed Saville-Smythe's name and address with Mr. Hamilton.

"What involvement do you have with Mr. Moore of Rottingdean?" Jones began.

"I act as Mr. Moore's solicitor in matters of purchasing properties and legal documents regarding his children."

"Do you act on behalf of Mr. Moore for his business dealings?"

"No, he has a London solicitor who deals with the business matters."

"Do you have a telephone in your home –number 52741?"

"Yes. It is my private line."

"What business do you conduct on that number?" There was no answer.

Jones continued, "Mr. Saville-Smythe as you know Post Office Telephones keep an accurate record of every call that any subscriber makes whether the number is listed or unlisted. We have checked your records with the telephone company and we are curious as to why so few calls are made from 52741, and why the calls that you do make are to repeated numbers? Please explain."

"I have nothing to say."

"Do you know a Thomas Napier of Hove?"

"Never heard of him."

"That's strange because the records state that you called his number several times a month ago."

"Show me that number"

Jones pointed to the telephone record. "The last call to this number was made a week before a robbery was committed in Rottingdean."

"So?"

"Mr. Napier, from that number, has admitted to committing that robbery and further has admitted that 52741 was the number that he had to call to set up communications with the man who ordered the robbery."

Finally Saville-Smythe spoke, "I had nothing to do with those attacks. I didn't even know that that young boy or the other chap were involved in the robbery until I received a call from Napier last week telling me about it."

"I have difficulty understanding how it was that you ordered the robbery yet you didn't know who was on the team."

"Because that is how I planned it. Nobody ever knows who puts up the money. I get someone like the Leader, Napier, to do the job."

"Well now your planning involves two murders and a beating. Perhaps that is what we should charge you with, accessory to murder."
Saville-Smythe attempted to get up as he aggressively protested his innocence of any violence.

"You can't do that. I had nothing to do with those crimes. I just told you."

"Well," said Jones, "perhaps it is time you told us everything that you have been involved in and then we could make a better decision on the charges."
Saville-Smythe looked at his solicitor and looking down at his hands began to recount the many times he had been responsible for ordering robberies. He gave dates, locations and which fences he had used to dispose of the articles. He added that Napier had organized several of the robberies,

"There was always someone ready to take the risk, but Napier was the best." He finished

"Is this why you picked him to rob Moore's house?"

"Yes. Napier didn't want to do it. He wanted out. But I talked him around and he agreed to do this last job for me"

"What was so special about the contents of Moore's safe that you wanted so badly?"

"Because it was a challenge. For several years there had been a rumour that somewhere in the south was a man who had amassed a fortune in jewels from smuggling. It was said that as soon as he was paid for delivery he converted the hard cash into jewellery and never used the same jeweller twice. I have been looking for this man ever since I learned about this cache. I paid good money for information and finally I knew that it had to be Moore. So I sent in a team."

"Do you have the jewels now?"

"Yes, at my home."

"Did you send to me a small box containing an antique brooch?"

Saville-Smythe nodded, "I felt so sick when Napier called and told me about the two murders. I knew that Moore had to be stopped even if eventually I myself became involved."

"That's all very well Mr. Saville-Smythe, but it's a bit late for Williams and Miller."

The officers left the room and the constable accompanied Saville-Smythe and his solicitor down to the holding cells. Although Jones was now fully aware of the events since the burglary there were still facts he needed to know. He found the Boss, Saville-Smythe, a very unlikable man but an intriguing character. How was it possible for a man such as him to lead a double life; a common criminal on one side and a respected family solicitor on the other? Why did the two sides come in contact with each other and was it revenge or just plain greed that bought about the nasty collision and a very messy ending. As for Moore, well Jones had taken an instant dislike to the man figuring him to be a ruthless bastard and he was a happy man to be proven right. Jones thought about Bobby and the life wasted just so that a greedy man could meet what he saw as a challenge. True, the robbery had been ordered by Saville-Smythe and he must share the blame for the deaths. But by stealing and then selling the snuffboxes Bobby had, indeed, precipitated a vengeful, murderous serious of events.

Jones knew that making the connection between Moore and the murders would be difficult. The two killers were still at large and Jones knew that he needed them in custody to put pressure on Moore. Smith had told him, with a wry grin that Moore had called in a solicitor, from another firm, and was still protesting that he was the victim not the criminal. Jones called Mac in London.

"We picked up Moore this morning. He went berserk with a gun. Moore found out that his own solicitor had double crossed him and Moore went after him with a gun."

There was a chuckle from the other end, "Well I was about to call you as we have something for you. It seems that the police knew someone was making a lot of money and Mitchell was questioned often but the police could never link him to the activity. By chance an old lag, just ready to be released from Wandsworth actually told a cellmate about the work he had done for Mitchell and that was reported to a prison officer. According to the report Mitchell had quite a large network of petty criminals working for him, including some enforcers. That's how we found out. But there's more, in his youth Mitchell was actually known as Higgins and operated down in the dockland area. He had a reputation of being very brutal to those that crossed him. Even as a youth he had a long string of alleged robberies and assaults to his name. He was only charged once and spent a few weeks in juvenile. You have caught a big fish my friend," laughed Mac.

"Wait 'til I tell my Sgt he will be so pleased. But we still haven't caught the two killers. Anything on them?"

"Oh Yes we have! We knew they were mates who hire themselves out as partners to the highest bidder, usually Mitchell. The big one, Herbert Mangle, was apprehended this morning at Victoria Station boarding the Dover train; the other was picked up two hours later catching a ferry to Ireland. We have them both and they have confessed to their part in your two murders and the beating. They have told us about Mitchell's London set-up and his involvement in your case, plus three more murders in London that Mitchell had ordered. One of the murders was that of a Mr Forest who was involved in Moore's diamond smuggling operation between London and Amsterdam. The print from the boy's dart box was very helpful as it turned out to be Mangle's and he had served time before."

"That's good news. Let us know when we can expect them down here. Now that this one is almost sewn up except for the paperwork, I'll be able to come up to discuss some ideas I have about the other matters."

"Look forward to it."

Jones hung up. Now that Mac had the two killers in custody he knew Moore was finished. The Scottish police found Sinclair hiding out in a small village just north of Edinburgh and he was on his way back to Brighton, under escort. Smith had been back out to Rottingdean and had reported that he and the local Sgt found a Morris car in the locked shed behind Moore's house and that in all likelihood was linked to the killings. Smith had confirmed that although the Morris was an older model it was in excellent running order and had been used recently.

But the jewels, mused Jones, who did they belong to? The insurance company who had possibly paid out compensation for their loss? Saville-Smythe had said that he had researched the pieces and found that most had been declared missing, lost or stolen during a robbery that hadn't been officially reported.

Jones had one more thing to do before he and Smith could go up to the hospital to see young Masters. Earlier Supt. Young had informed Jones that the Chief Constable was on his way into the station and that he, the C.C., demanded that Jones give him an update on the case before leaving. Jones left his office and walked down to the conference room. He could hear the buzz of conversation even before he opened the door onto a room full of uniformed policeman, CID and others. Smith stood to one side near the front and as Jones looked over Smith smiled and looked away.

Supt. Young called for quiet, gave a few introductory remarks about the C.C. and then asked Jones to take over.

"I know that every one of you present has been involved in this case, which I shall refer to as the Bobby Williams' case. So I asked Supt. Young to invite you here for this de-briefing, that way each of you will know the current status of this case. First of all we have Mr. Saville-Smyth, solicitor, in custody and he will be charged with organizing a series of robberies that have plagued the southern region for almost two years. Robberies to which, I might add, he has confessed. Mr. Saville-Smythe has also confessed to ordering the robbery of Mr.

Moore's house but as yet we can find nothing to link him to the murders of Bobby Williams or Ted Miller or the beating of Thomas Napier, who were the actual burglars. We are also looking into his possible involvement with the recent robberies in the country houses."

Jones picked up another sheet of notes and then looked across at the C.C and then to Smith.

"We have another person presently in custody, a Mr. Alex Moore, of Rottingdean, alias Mr. Mitchell of London, also known as Mr. Higgins of London. This man will be charged with the following: the murders of both Bobby Williams and Ted Miller, the attempted murder of Constable Masters, the attempted murder of Thomas Napier, assault causing bodily harm-three counts." There was silence in the room as each officer realized the ramifications of these charges. "You will be pleased to know that Constable Masters is recovering in hospital and is looking forward to visitors. Sgt Smith and I are headed up there as soon as we are finished here. Also, I have a report from Inspector MacDonald of Scotland Yard that they have two London men in custody and each has confessed to being responsible, with Moore, for the deaths of Williams and Miller and the beating of Napier."

Jones looked around, "Finally I want to thank all of you for the extra effort and time that you have put in on this case and warn you to be prepared for the horde of reporters that this case will attract. Remember Supt. Young or myself will be the only spokespeople regarding this case so please do not be tempted to say anything that might jeopardize the prosecution of this case. Thank you." With that Jones looked at Smith and together they left the room.

"Up to see Masters now?" asked Smith.

"Yes, but afterwards I would like to go on to visit Mr. and Mrs. Williams to let them know what happened today. Will you come?" Just then there was a knock at Jones' door and Supt. Young poked his head around the door.

"Just called in to offer my congratulations and let you know how much I enjoyed the meeting." Chuckling the Super slowly closed the door behind him.

The visit to Masters was not very long, doctor's orders, but long enough for Smith to let Masters know how the chase had finished, that his name would be put in for a Police Commendation medal and that his colleagues would be up soon to see him.

Mr. and Mrs. Williams welcomed the officers into their home and were pleased that the murderers had been caught but as Mrs. Williams quietly asked

"What good will that do now, our Bobby is gone and our lives will never be the same again." Both sat very quietly listening to Jones as he relayed the events of that day. The officers quietly let themselves out of the front door and walked silently to the car.

"She is absolutely right of course all we can do is hope that justice will be done," said Smith climbing into the driver's seat. It was a few minutes until either one spoke. Then turning to Smith Jones said,

"There are two more victims in this case Jack, Moore's two young children. It will be so hard on them. No mother and father in prison. We must make enquiries to see if their mother had any relations who could take them in .Otherwise they will have to go into Care. Again it is the innocent who will suffer terrible consequences of others greed." Smith nodded in agreement.

It was later as they were enjoying a pint at the King and Queen that Smith asked Jones.

"What was the Super on about when he said he enjoyed this afternoon's meeting?"

"You know that the Super and the C.C. do not see eye to eye on policing methods?" explained Jones.

"Yes."

"Well it seems our illustrious C.C had dinner a couple of weeks ago at a certain house in Rottingdean and not only did he sit down with the host Mr. Moore, but Saville-Smythe was also a guest."

"Oh that's rich, I'll drink to that!!

THE END

Manufactured by Amazon.ca
Bolton, ON

33213345R00107